Samuel French Acting Edition

Sticks and Bones

by David Rabe

SAMUELFRENCH.COM   SAMUELFRENCH.CO.UK

FOR PRODUCTION ENQUIRIES

UNITED STATES AND CANADA
Info@SamuelFrench.com
1-866-598-8449

UNITED KINGDOM AND EUROPE
Plays@SamuelFrench.co.uk
020-7255-4302

Each title is subject to availability from Samuel French, depending upon country of performance. Please be aware that *STICKS AND BONES* may not be licensed by Samuel French in your territory. Professional and amateur producers should contact the nearest Samuel French office or licensing partner to verify availability.

MUSIC USE NOTE

Licensees are solely responsible for obtaining formal written permission from copyright owners to use copyrighted music in the performance of this play and are strongly cautioned to do so. If no such permission is obtained by the licensee, then the licensee must use only original music that the licensee owns and controls. Licensees are solely responsible and liable for all music clearances and shall indemnify the copyright owners of the play(s) and their licensing agent, Samuel French, against any costs, expenses, losses and liabilities arising from the use of music by licensees. Please contact the appropriate music licensing authority in your territory for the rights to any incidental music.

IMPORTANT BILLING AND CREDIT REQUIREMENTS

If you have obtained performance rights to this title, please refer to your licensing agreement for important billing and credit requirements.

The revised version of ***STICKS AND BONES*** was first produced by The New Group at The Pershing Square Signature Center on November 6, 2014. The performance was directed by Scott Elliot, with sets by Derek McLane, costumes by Susan Hilferty, lights by Peter Kaczorowski, and projections by Olivia Sebesky. The cast was as follows:

OZZIE	Bill Pullman
HARRIET	Holly Hunter
RICK	Raviv Ullman
DAVID	Ben Schnetzer
SERGEANT MAJOR	Morocco Omari
ZUNG	Nadia Gan
FATHER DONALD	Richard Chamberlain

STICKS AND BONES was first produced by The New York Shakespeare Festival, at The Public Theater on November 7, 1971. The performance was directed by Jeff Bleckner, with sets by Santo Loquasto, costumes by Theoni V. Aldredge, lights by Ian Calderon, and slides photographed by Joseph Linsalata. The cast was as follows:

OZZIE	Tom Aldredge
HARRIET	Elizabeth Wilson
RICK	Cliff De Young
DAVID	Drew Snyder
SERGEANT MAJOR	Hector Elias
ZUNG	Asa Gim
FATHER DONALD	Charles Siebert

CHARACTERS

OZZIE

HARRIET

RICK

DAVID

SERGEANT MAJOR

ZUNG

FATHER DONALD

SETTING

The Family Home.

TIME

Autumn.

ACT ONE

(The set is an American home circa 1970, a quality of brightness. Dining room table upstage. A couch faces out, with a coffee table in front of it, and armchair to the side. On stage right, stairs go up to a landing that is beside a bedroom visible to the audience, a boy's bedroom, with a bed, a dresser, some trophies. The stairs, after branching off to the right, continue up to the attic. Stage left of the living room has the front door with a coat rack on the side. Stage left has a swinging door which is the kitchen door. Lights up. The TV is on, murmuring. OZZIE, HARRIET, and FATHER DONALD are seated on the couch with OZZIE in the middle. FATHER DONALD holds a basketball.)

FATHER DONALD. A feel for it is the big thing, Ozzie. A feel for the ball. You know, they're bouncing it; dribbling it. They don't even look at it.

> *(Telephone rings.)*

OZZIE. I'll get it.

> *(Moving past FATHER DONALD toward the phone.)*

Excuse me.

FATHER DONALD. *(Standing.)* You can do it, Harriet. Give it a try.

OZZIE. *(Into the phone.)* – Hello? –

> *(As HARRIET stands, FATHER DONALD bounces the ball to her, and she catches it, fearfully, squealing.)*

FATHER DONALD. That a girl – Go on, Harriet. Give it a try. Let's see you bounce it. Let's see you dribble it.

(She gives it a try, kind of dropping it.)

HARRIET. – Oh, Father.

OZZIE. *(Hanging up.)* Nobody there.

FATHER DONALD. *(Retrieving the ball.)* That's what I'm telling you. You gotta help kids. Keep 'em outta trouble. We help organize sports activities; it does 'em a world a good. You know that. And they need you.

OZZIE. Well, I was a decent basketball player – I could get around, but my strong suit was track and field. I was quite a miler. Dash man, too. I told you, Father. I could throw the discus.

> *(As* **OZZIE** *strikes the pose of a discus thrower, the telephone rings, and he runs for the phone.)*

FATHER DONALD. But this is basketball season.

> *(***FATHER DONALD** *moves to* **HARRIET** *and they go toward the door as* **OZZIE,** *at the phone, says "Hello," then listens intently.)*

You listen to me, Harriet, you get that husband of yours out there to help us. It'll do him good and he's the kind of man we need. Leaders. We need leaders.

HARRIET. Oh, Father Donald, bless me.

FATHER DONALD. Of course.

> *(Blessing her, holding the ball.)*

See you on the court Ozzie. Bye-bye.

HARRIET. *(As* **FATHER DONALD** *goes.)* Goodbye, Father.

> *(Turning to look for a moment at* **OZZIE.***)*

Why aren't you talking?

> *(Silence: she is looking at him.)*

Ozzie, why aren't you talking?

OZZIE. *(Slowly lowering the phone.)* They're gone. They hung up.

HARRIET. You didn't say a word. You said nothing.

OZZIE. I said my name.

HARRIET. What did they want?

OZZIE. I said hello.

HARRIET. Were they selling something – is that what they wanted?

OZZIE. No, no.

HARRIET. Well…who was it?

OZZIE. What?

HARRIET. What are we talking about?

OZZIE. The Government. It was…you know…

HARRIET. Ozzie! No.

> *(Fearful.)*

OZZIE. No, he's all right, he's coming home!

HARRIET. Why didn't you let me speak? Who was it?

OZZIE. No, no.

HARRIET. It was David.

OZZIE. No. Somebody else. Some clerk. I don't know who.

HARRIET. You're lying.

OZZIE. No. There was just all this static – it was hard to hear. But he was coming home was part of it, and they had his records and papers but I couldn't talk to him directly even though he was right there, standing right there.

HARRIET. I don't understand.

OZZIE. That's what they said…and he was fine and everything. And he wanted them to say "Hello" for him. He'd lost some weight. He would be sent by truck. I could hear truck engines in the background – revving. They wanted to know my name. I told them.

HARRIET. No more?

OZZIE. They were very professional. Very brusque…

HARRIET. No more…at all…?

> *(As the door opens and* **RICK** *comes in. He is young, seventeen. His clothing is neat and up-to-date. He carries a guitar and camera.)*

RICK. *(Very cheerful.)* Hi, Mom, hi, Dad.

(**RICK** *heads speedily to the kitchen.*)

HARRIET. *(Cheerful.)* Hi, Rick.

OZZIE. *(Cheerful.)* Hi, Rick.

(**RICK** *is all the way into the kitchen when* **HARRIET** *squeals.*)

HARRIET. Ohhh, Ricky, Ricky, your brother's on his way home. David's coming home!

OZZIE. We just got a call.

RICK. Ohhh, boy!

HARRIET. Isn't that wonderful? Isn't it? Your father talked to him. Oh, I bet you're starving, sit, sit.

OZZIE. I talked to somebody, Rick.

HARRIET. There's fudge and ice cream in the fridge. Would you like that?

RICK. Oh, yeah and could I have some pop?

(She is on her way to the kitchen, nodding.)

Wow, that sure is some news. I'm awful hungry.

OZZIE. Never had a doubt. A boy like that – if he leaves, he comes back.

RICK. How about me? What if I left?

(As he picks up a comic book.)

OZZIE. Absolutely. Absolutely.

(Silence: **RICK** *reads the comic.)*

I built jeeps, tanks, trucks.

RICK. What?

OZZIE. In the other war, I mean. Number Two. I worked on vehicles. Vehicles were needed, and I worked to build them. Sometimes I put on wheels, tightened 'em up. I never…served…is what I mean. They got all those people – soldiers, Rick – you see what I mean? They got 'em across the ocean, they don't have any jeeps or tanks or trucks, what are they gonna do, stand around? Wait for a bus on the beachhead? Call a cab?

RICK. No public transportation in a war.

OZZIE. That's right, that's right.

> (*As* **HARRIET** *enters, carrying fudge and ice cream.*)

HARRIET. Oh, Ozzie, Ozzie, do you remember – I just remembered that time David locked himself in that old icebox. We didn't know where he was. We looked all over. We couldn't find him. And then there was this icebox in this clearing…out in the middle. I'll bet you don't even remember.

OZZIE. Of course I remember.

HARRIET. And he leaped to us. So frightened.

OZZIE. He couldn't even speak – he couldn't even speak – just these noises.

HARRIET. Or that time he fell from that tree.

OZZIE. My God, he was somethin'. If he wasn't fallin', he was gettin' hit.

HARRIET. And there was that day we went out into the woods. It was just all wind and clouds. We sailed a kite!

OZZIE. I'd nearly forgotten.

RICK. Where was I?

HARRIET. You were just a baby, Rick. We had a picnic.

RICK. I'm gonna get some more pop, okay?

> (**HARRIET** *touches him as he passes.*)

OZZIE. What a day that was. I felt great that day.

HARRIET. And then Hank came along. He came from out of the woods wanting to be with us –

OZZIE. That's right. I miss that rascal, Hank Grenweller – what a buddy he was.

HARRIET. He was happy that day.

OZZIE. We were all happy. And then we had that race. Wasn't that the day?

HARRIET. I don't remember.

OZZIE. Hank and me! Hank Grenweller. A footrace. And I beat him. I did it; got him.

HARRIET. Noooo.

OZZIE. It was only inches, but –

HARRIET. You know that's not true. If it was close – that race you ran – and it was – *(With nostalgia and fondness.)* I remember now – it was because he let it be close – no other reason. We were all having fun. He didn't want to make you feel badly.

RICK. *(His head poking out of the kitchen.)* You people want some fudge?

HARRIET. No, Rick.

OZZIE. No, thanks.

> *(Back to* **HARRIET.***)*

I don't know he didn't try. I don't know that.

> *(As* **RICK** *returns, eating, and settling onto the couch with his guitar.)*

HARRIET. I think I'll be going up to bed; take a little nap.

RICK. Sleepy, Mom?

HARRIET. A little.

RICK. That's a good idea then.

HARRIET. Call me.

RICK. Okay.

HARRIET. Do you know, the day he left? It was a winter day. November, Ozzie.

> *(Moving up the stairs.)*

OZZIE. I know.

HARRIET. I prayed, I prayed and now he's home.

OZZIE. It was a winter day.

HARRIET. I know.

RICK. 'Night, Mom.

> *(He is toying with his guitar. He looks up when she doesn't answer and yells.)*

'Night, Mom!

HARRIET. *(From offstage.)* 'Night Rick! Turn off the TV, somebody.

(**RICK** *crosses to the TV. He turns it off and starts to the armchair.* **OZZIE** *watches. Silence.*)

OZZIE. I knew she was praying. She moves her lips.

(**RICK** *begins, softly, to strum and tune the guitar.*)

I mean they got seventeen hundred million men they gotta deal with, how they gonna do that without any trucks and tanks and jeeps? But I'm some kinda jerk because I wasn't out there blastin' away, huh? I was useful. I put my time to use. I been in fights. Fat Kramer. How we used to fight. Black eyes. Bloody noses. That's all we did.

(**RICK** *strums some notes on his guitar.*)

How come I'm so restless? I…seen him do some awful, awful things, ole Dave. He was a mean… Foul-tempered little baby. I'm only glad I was here when they sent him off to do his killing. That's right.

(*Silence.*)

I feel like I swallowed ants, that's how restless I am. Outran a bowlin' ball one time.

These guys bet me I couldn't do it and I did, beat it to the pins. Got a runnin' start, then the –

(*A loud knocking makes him jump up, glancing at the door and then away, and at* **RICK**.)

Did you do that?

RICK. Somebody knockin'.

OZZIE. Knockin'?

RICK. The door, Dad.

OZZIE. Oh.

RICK. You want me to get it?

OZZIE. No, no. It's just so late.

RICK. That's all right.

OZZIE. Sure.

(*He opens the door. But the door is thrust open and a black man, formidable in the dress green uniform of a* **SERGEANT MAJOR**, *lots of ribbons, wearing a Garrison cap, steps in.)*

SERGEANT MAJOR. Excuse me. Listen to me. I'd like to speak to the father here. I'd like to know who...is the father? Could...you tell me the address?

OZZIE. May I ask who it is who's asking?

SERGEANT MAJOR. I am. I'm asking. What's the address of this house?

OZZIE. But I mean, who is it that wants to know?

SERGEANT MAJOR. We called; we spoke. Is this 717 Dunbar?

OZZIE. Yes.

SERGEANT MAJOR. What's wrong with you?

OZZIE. Don't you worry about me.

SERGEANT MAJOR. I have your son.

OZZIE. What?

SERGEANT MAJOR. Your son.

OZZIE. No.

SERGEANT MAJOR. But he is. I have papers, pictures, prints. I know your blood and his. This is the right address. Please. Excuse me.

(He pivots, steps out into the dark.)

I am very busy. I have your father, David.

(After a moment, there is the tapping of a long, red-tipped cane in the shadows, then in the door, as **DAVID**, *twenty-five or so, wearing sunglasses and a uniform of dress greens, enters. He carries a duffle bag, and moves, probing the air, as the* **SERGEANT MAJOR** *returns behind* **DAVID**.)

OZZIE. Dave?

SERGEANT MAJOR. He's blind.

OZZIE. What?

SERGEANT MAJOR. Blind.

OZZIE. I don't understand.

SERGEANT MAJOR. We're very sorry.

OZZIE. Ohhhhh. Yes. Ohhhh.

 (Realizing.)

I see...sure. I mean, we didn't know. Nobody said it. I mean, sure, Dave, sure; it's all right – don't you worry. Rick's here too, Dave – Rick, your brother, tell him "Hello."

RICK. *(Cheery.)* Hi, Dave.

DAVID. You said "Father."

OZZIE. Well, there's two of us, Dave. Two.

DAVID. Sergeant, you said "home." I don't think so.

OZZIE. Dave, sure.

DAVID. It doesn't feel right.

OZZIE. But it is, Dave – me and Rick – Dad and Rick; and Mom. Harriet!

 (Calling upstairs.)

Harriet!

DAVID. Let me touch their faces... I can't see. Let me put my fingers on their faces.

OZZIE. What? Do what?

SERGEANT MAJOR. Will that be all right, if he does that?

OZZIE. Sure... Sure... Fine.

SERGEANT MAJOR. *(Helping DAVID to OZZIE.)* It will take him time.

OZZIE. That's normal and to be expected. I'm not surprised. Not at all. We figured on this. Sure, we did. Didn't we, Rick?

RICK. *(Occupied with his camera, an Instamatic.)* I wanna take some pictures. How are you Dave?

DAVID. What room is this?

OZZIE. Middle room, Dave. TV room. TV's in –

HARRIET. David. Oh, David.

 (Hurrying down the stairs.)

David...

 *(**OZZIE** hurries toward **HARRIET**, stopping her before she can get to **DAVID**.)*

OZZIE. Harriet, don't be upset…they say… Harriet, Harriet… He can't see… Harriet…they say – he can't… see. That man.

HARRIET. Can't see? What do you mean?

SERGEANT MAJOR. He's blind.

HARRIET. No. Who says? No, no.

OZZIE. Look at him; he looks so old… But it's nothing, Harriet, I'm sure.

SERGEANT MAJOR. I hope you people understand.

OZZIE. It's probably just how he's tired from his long trip.

HARRIET. Oh, you're home now, David. You're home.

SERGEANT MAJOR. *(With a large sheet of paper waving in his hands, maybe on a clipboard.)* Who's gonna sign this for me? It's a shipping receipt. I got to have somebody's signature to show you got him. I got to have somebody's name on the paper.

OZZIE. Let me. All right?

SERGEANT MAJOR. Just here, here, here, and here and here, you see? Your name or mark.

> *(As they move toward the coffee table to sit and sign.)*

OZZIE. Fine, listen, would you like some refreshments?

SERGEANT MAJOR. No.

OZZIE. I mean while I do this. Cake and coffee. Of course you do.

SERGEANT MAJOR. No.

OZZIE. Sure.

SERGEANT MAJOR. *(Leaning back, exhausted, almost in a reverie.)* No. I haven't time. I've got to get going. I've got trucks out there backed up for blocks. Other boys. I got to get on to Chicago and some of them to Denver and Cleveland, Reno, New Orleans, Boston, Trenton, Watts, Atlanta. And when I get back they'll be layin' all over the grass; layin' there in pieces all over the grass, their backs been broken, their brains jellied, their insides turned into garbage. No-legged boys and one-legged boys. I'm due in Harlem; I got to get to the Bronx and Queens, Cincinnati, St. Louis, Reading. I don't have time for coffee. I got deliveries to make all across this country.

DAVID. Noooooo...

> *(His hands on* **HARRIET** *'s face, a kind of realization, terrified. He is desperate to get back to the* **SERGEANT**.*)*

Sergeant, noo; there's something wrong; it all feels wrong. Where are you? Are you here? I don't know these people!

SERGEANT MAJOR. That's natural, soldier; it's natural you feel that way.

DAVID. Nooooo.

HARRIET. David! Just sit, be still.

DAVID. Don't you hear me?

OZZIE. Harriet, calm him.

DAVID. The air is wrong; the smells and sounds, the wind.

HARRIET. David, please, please. What is it? Be still. Please...

DAVID. God damn you, Sergeant, I am lonely here! I am lonely!

SERGEANT MAJOR. I got to go.

DAVID. Sergeant!

> *(***DAVID*** is clutching at the* **SERGEANT MAJOR**, *who pulls free, knocking* **DAVID** *to the floor.)*

SERGEANT MAJOR. YOU SHUT UP! YOU PISS-ASS SOLDIER, YOU SHUT THE FUCK UP!

OZZIE. Listen, let me walk you to the door. All right? I'd like to take a look at that truck of yours. All right?

SERGEANT MAJOR. There's more than one.

OZZIE. Fine.

SERGEANT MAJOR. It's a convoy.

OZZIE. Good.

(They exit, and **RICK**, *making his way to the door, looks out.)*

RICK. Sure are lots of trucks, Mom!

HARRIET. Are there?

RICK. Oh, yeah. Gonna rain some more, too.

HARRIET. Is it?

RICK. Yeah.

(Bounding up the stairs.)

See you in the morning. Night, Dave.

HARRIET. It's good to have you here again; so good to see you. You look…just…fine. You must be so relieved to be out of there – to be –

*(**OZZIE** has come in the front door and she senses his presence behind her.)*

He bewilders you, doesn't he.

OZZIE. What? No. Uh-uh.

HARRIET. Of course he does.

*(**OZZIE** heads for the stairs, grabbing the fallen duffle bag…)*

Where are you going? You thought you knew what was right, all those years, didn't you, teaching him sports and fighting.

*(**OZZIE** stops; he doesn't know.)*

Do you understand what I'm trying to say? A mother knows things… A father cannot ever know them. The measles, chickenpox, cuts and bruises. Never have you come upon him in the night as he lay awake and staring…praying.

OZZIE. I saw him put a knife through the skin of a cat. I saw him cut the belly open.

DAVID. Nooooo…

HARRIET. David, David…

DAVID. *(Accusatory.)* Ricky, Ricky.

HARRIET. He's gone to bed.

DAVID. I want to leave.

(Falling into a complete, almost infantile panic.)

HARRIET. What is it?

DAVID. Help me.

OZZIE. Settle down! Relax.

DAVID. I want to leave! I want to leave! I want to leave. I –

(As he smashes into something, goes down, flails his cane.)

– want to leave.

OZZIE & HARRIET. Dave! David! Davey!

DAVID. …to leave! Please.

(He is on the floor, fearful, but trying to be quiet.)

HARRIET. Ozzie, get him some medicine. He needs some medicine. Get him some Easy Sleep.

OZZIE. Good idea.

HARRIET. It's in the medicine cabinet; a little blue bottle, little pink pills.

OZZIE. I'll be right back.

(He hurries up the stairway and off down the hall.)

HARRIET. *(Kneeling with* **DAVID.***)* It'll give you sleep you need, David; the sleep you remember. You're our child and you're home. Our good…beautiful boy.

DAVID. *(Pushing away from her.)* Help me! Help me! Help me!

(And the front door is pushed open. There is a small girl in the doorway, peering in, about to enter, an Asian girl, **ZUNG.** *She wears the Vietnamese Ao Dai. As* **HARRIET** *bolts over, shoving the door closed with the girl on the outside.)*

HARRIET. Oh, my goodness.

(Turning out, her back pressed to the door.)

What an awful…wind.

(Blackout. Music.)

Scene Two

(Lights. A match flickers as **HARRIET** *lights a candle.* **OZZIE** *is asleep, sitting up in a chair. As* **HARRIET** *moves toward him, stands over him,* **OZZIE** *startles.)*

HARRIET. Oh! I didn't mean to wake you. I lit a candle so I wouldn't wake you.

(Beat.)

I'm sorry.

OZZIE. I wasn't sleeping.

HARRIET. I thought you were.

OZZIE. Couldn't. Tried. Couldn't. Thinking. Thoughts running very fast. Trying to remember the night David…was…well…made… You know. Do you understand me? I don't know why. But the feeling was in me that I had to figure something out and if only I could remember that night, the mood… I would be able. You're shaking your head.

HARRIET. I don't understand.

OZZIE. No. Well… I don't either.

(Turning on a flashlight, he waves it about.)

I'm going to look around outside. I heard a sound before. Like mice in the walls.

HARRIET. We don't have any mice.

OZZIE. I know. I'm just going to look around.

(He opens the door. **ZUNG** *is still standing there. As* **OZZIE**, *with his flashlight, goes out, she steps in before he can close it.)*

HARRIET. Good night. Let me know what you find.

*(***DAVID*** sits up in his bed.)*

DAVID. Who's there? Who's there?

(Standing.)

Is someone there? Cho Co. Cho Ung?

(HARRIET stares up, having heard him. She moves toward the stairs, climbing softly.)

Are you there? Is someone there? Cho Co. Zung? Zung? Zung?

(ZUNG moves through the living room, as HARRIET raps softly on DAVID's door, using their special knock which requires a response. DAVID does not respond, and she knocks again, and then she opens the door. DAVID lies on the bed... Meanwhile, ZUNG climbs the stairs from the living room to the landing, very quietly.)

HARRIET. I heard you call.

DAVID. What?

HARRIET. I heard you call.

DAVID. I didn't.

HARRIET. Would you like a glass of warm milk?

DAVID. I was sleeping.

HARRIET. How about that milk? Would you like some milk?

(Slowly, ZUNG makes her way toward DAVID's room.)

DAVID. I didn't call. I was sleeping.

HARRIET. You're troubled; warm milk would help. Do you pray at all anymore? If I were to pray now, would you pray with me?

DAVID. What...do you want?

HARRIET. Their skins are yellow, aren't they? They eat the flesh of dogs.

DAVID. I know. I've seen them.

HARRIET. Pray with me; pray.

DAVID. What do you want?

HARRIET. Just to talk, that's all. Just to know that you're home and safe again. Nothing else; only that we're all together, a family. You must be exhausted. Don't worry; sleep. Good night.

(A whisper; she blows out the candle and goes. **ZUNG** *enters* **DAVID**'s *room as* **HARRIET** *goes out, and* **DAVID** *bolts up, sensing someone there. Frightened.)*

(Blackout. Music.)

Scene Three

(Lights up. It is a bright afternoon, and OZZIE, *with a screwdriver in hand, pokes about the TV set.)*

OZZIE. C'mon, c'mon. Ohhhh, c'mon, this one more win, one more victory, and Ole State is tournament bound. C'mon, what is it. Ohh, hey… Darn. Ohhhhhh.

*(*HARRIET *enters, carrying a glass of orange juice.)*

HARRIET. Ozzie, take this up to David, make him drink it.

OZZIE. Harriet, the TV is broke.

HARRIET. What?

OZZIE. There's picture but no sound. I don't –

(Grabbing her by the arm, pulling her toward the TV.)

HARRIET. Stoppit, you're spilling the juice.

(Pulling free.)

OZZIE. It's Saturday. I want to watch it. I turned it on, picture came on just like normal. I got the volume up full blast.

(Having set the juice down on the coffee table, HARRIET *pulls the screwdriver from his hand and turns off the TV.)*

Hey! I want to fix it!

HARRIET. I want to talk about David.

OZZIE. David's all right.

(Picking up the phone book.)

I'm gonna call the repairman.

HARRIET. *(Following him, taking the phone book from him.)* Ozzie, he won't eat. He just lays there. I offer him food, he won't eat it. No, no. The TV repairman won't help, you silly. He doesn't matter. There's something wrong with David. He's been home days and days and still he speaks only when spoken to; there is no bounce in his step, no smile, he's not happy to be here and not once has he touched me sweetly or held me, and I don't think he's even shaken your hand. Has he shaken your hand?

(**OZZIE** *flops down on the couch.*)

OZZIE. Oh, I don't mind that. Why should I mind –

HARRIET. And now he's talking to himself! What about that? Do you mind that? He mutters in his sleep.

OZZIE. Ohhh, noooo.

HARRIET. Yes. And it's not a regular kind of talking at all. It's very strange – very spooky.

OZZIE. Spooky?

HARRIET. That's right.

OZZIE. I never heard him.

HARRIET. You sleep too deeply. I took a candle and followed the sound. I was in his room. He lay there, speaking.

OZZIE. He was speaking? Speaking what?

HARRIET. I don't know. I couldn't understand.

OZZIE. Was it words?

HARRIET. All kind of funny and fast.

OZZIE. Maybe prayer; I bet he was praying.

HARRIET. No. No, it was secret. Oh, Ozzie, I know praying when I hear it, and it wasn't praying he was doing. We meant our son to be so different from this – I don't understand – good and strong. And yet...he is. I know he is. But there are moments when I see him... hiding...in that bed behind those awful glasses...and I see the chalkiness that's come into his skin, the –

OZZIE. Those glasses are simply to ease his discomfort.

HARRIET. I hate them.

OZZIE. They're tinted glass and plastic – Don't be so damn suspicious.

HARRIET. I'm not, I'm not. It's seeing I'm doing, not suspicion. Suspicion hasn't any reasons. It's you – now accusing me for no reason when I'm only worried.

(*As* OZZIE *reaches for the glass of juice, she grabs the juice, very protectively.*)

No, no, that's for David.

OZZIE. I want some juice.

HARRIET. This is for him. He needs his nourishment.

OZZIE. I want a little juice, Harriet.

HARRIET. Shut up. You're selfish. You're so selfish.

OZZIE. I'll walk over there; I'll pour it on the floor. I'll break the glass.

HARRIET. A few years ago you might have done that kind of thing.

OZZIE. I didn't get much sleep last night. You woke me up with all your snorting and snoggling around. I woke up and I looked at you and all I could see was the lovely way you looked when you were young; and there you were, struggling to breathe. You were trying to breathe.

(*Handing over the juice.*)

What do you give me when you give me this?

HARRIET. Your juice. And I always looked pretty much the way I do now. I never looked much different.

(DAVID *appears upstairs.*)

DAVID. Good morning.

HARRIET. Good morning!

(*He descends toward them dressed in a robe.*)

OZZIE. Oh, David, ohhh, good morning. Hello. How do you feel this fine bright morning; how do you feel?

DAVID. He was a big man, wasn't he?

OZZIE. What?

DAVID. Hank. You were talking about Hank Grenweller. I thought you were.

OZZIE. Oh, yes. Hank. Very big. Big. A good fine friend, ole Hank.

DAVID. You felt when he was with you he filled the room.

> *(As **DAVID**, searching with his cane, and with some help, makes his way to sit in the armchair.)*

OZZIE. It was the way he talked that did that. He boomed. His voice just boomed.

DAVID. He was here once and you wanted me to sit on his lap, isn't that right? It was after dinner. He was in a chair in the corner.

HARRIET. That's right.

DAVID. His hand was gone – the bone showed in the skin.

OZZIE. My God, what a memory – did you hear that, Harriet? You were only four or five. He'd just had this terrible awful auto accident. His hand was hurt, not gone.

DAVID. No. It was congenital.

OZZIE. What?

DAVID. That hand. The sickness in it.

OZZIE. Congenital?

DAVID. I'd like some coffee.

HARRIET. Of course. And what else with it?

DAVID. Nothing.

HARRIET. Oh, no, no, you've got to eat. To get back your strength. You must. Pancakes? How do pancakes sound?

> *(Darting in the kitchen swinging door and right back out.)*

Or wheat cakes? Or there's eggs? And juice? Orange or prune; or waffles.

> *(Darting in the kitchen swinging door and right back out.)*

I bet it's eggs you want. Over, David? Over easy? Or my specialty scrambled?

DAVID. I'm only thirsty.

HARRIET. Well, all right then, coffee is what you'll have and I'll just put some eggs on the side; you used to love them so, remember?

> *(Darting into the kitchen.)*

OZZIE. I mean, I hate to harp on a thing, but I just think you're way off base on Hank, Dave. I just think you're dead wrong.

DAVID. He told me.

OZZIE. Who?

DAVID. Hank.

OZZIE. You talked to Hank?

DAVID. In California. The day before they shipped me overseas.

OZZIE. No, no. He went to Georgia when he left here. We have all his letters postmarked Georgia.

DAVID. It was California. I was in the barracks. The CQ came to tell me there was someone to see me. It was Hank asking did I remember him. He'd seen my name on a list and wondered if I was Ozzie's boy. He was dying, he said. The sickness was congenital. We had a long, long talk.

OZZIE. But his parents were good fine people, David.

DAVID. Don't you understand? We spoke.

OZZIE. Did he wanna know about me? Did he mention me?

DAVID. He asked…how you were.

OZZIE. Well, I'm fine. Sure. You told him. Fine. Fine.

HARRIET. *(Entering with a cup of coffee.)* It must be so wonderful for you to be home. It must just be so wonderful. A little strange, maybe…just a little, but time will take care of all that. It always does. You get sick and you don't know how you're going to get better and then you do. You just do. You must have terrible, awful, ugly dreams, though.

> *(Silence.)*

OZZIE. She said you probably have terrible awful ugly dreams...though.

DAVID. What?

HARRIET. Don't you remember when we spoke the other night?

DAVID. Who?

HARRIET. You called to me and then you claimed you hadn't.

DAVID. I didn't.

HARRIET. Ohhh, we had a lovely conversation, David. Of course you called. You called, we talked. We talked and laughed and it was very pleasant. Could I see behind your glasses?

DAVID. What? Do...what?

HARRIET. See behind your glasses; see your eyes.

OZZIE. Me too, Dave; could we?

DAVID. My eyes are...ugly.

OZZIE. We don't mind.

HARRIET. We're your parents, David.

DAVID. I don't want you to.

OZZIE. And something else I've been meaning to ask you – Why did you cry out against us that first night – to that stranger, I mean, that sergeant?

HARRIET. And you do dream. You do.

OZZIE. Sure. You needn't be ashamed.

HARRIET. We all do it. All of us.

OZZIE. We have things that haunt us.

HARRIET. And it would mean nothing at all – it would be of no consequence at all – if only you didn't speak.

DAVID. I don't understand.

OZZIE. She says she heard you, Dave.

HARRIET. I stood outside your door.

DAVID. No.

OZZIE. A terrible experience for her, Dave; you can see that.

HARRIET. Whatever it is, David, tell us.

OZZIE. What's wrong?

DAVID. No.

HARRIET. We'll work it out.

OZZIE. You can't know how you hurt us. Not until you have children of your own.

DAVID. I wasn't asleep.

HARRIET. What? Not…asleep…?

DAVID. No. No. I was awake; lying awake and speaking.

OZZIE. Now wait a minute.

DAVID. Someone was with me – there in the dark – I don't know what's wrong with me – but I feel, I feel –

HARRIET. There's nothing wrong with you. It was me. I was with you.

DAVID. No. In my room. I could feel it. Someone else.

HARRIET. I was there.

DAVID. No.

OZZIE. Harriet, wait!

HARRIET. What are you saying, "Wait"? I was there.

OZZIE. Oh, my God. Oh, Christ, of course. Oh, Dave, forgive us.

HARRIET. What?

OZZIE. Dave, I understand. It's buddies left behind.

DAVID. What?

OZZIE. Maybe your mother can't, but I can. Men serving together in war, it's a powerful thing – and I don't mean to sound like I think I know it – all of it, I mean – I don't, I couldn't. But I respect you having had it. I almost envy you having had it, Dave. I mean true… comradeship.

DAVID. Dad…

OZZIE. I had just a taste. Not that those trucks and factory were any battlefield, but there was a taste of it there – in the jokes we told and the way we saw each other first in the morning. We told dirty filthy jokes, Dave, we shot

pool, played cards, drank beer late every night, singing
all these crazy songs.

DAVID. That's not it, Dad.

OZZIE. But all that's nothing, I'm sure, to what it must be
in war. The things you must touch and see. Honor. And
then one of you is hurt, wounded, made blind – he has
to leave his buddies.

DAVID. No. Not my buddies.

OZZIE. What is it then?

DAVID. I had fear of all the kinds of dying that there are
when I went from here, and then there was this girl…
with hands and hair like wings. There were candles
above the net of gauze under which we lay. Lizards.
Cannon could be heard. A girl to weigh no more than
dust.

HARRIET. A nurse, right… David?

OZZIE. No, no, no, Harriet. One of them foreign
correspondents, English maybe, or French.

HARRIET. Oh, how lovely! A WAC or Red Cross girl…?

DAVID. No.

OZZIE. Redhead or blonde, Dave?

DAVID. No.

OZZIE. I mean, all right, what you mean is you whored
around a lot. Sure. You whored around. That's what
you're saying. You banged some whores – had some
intercourse. Sure, I mean, that's my point. You shacked
up with. I mean, hit on. Hit on, Dave. Dicked. Look at
me. I mean, you pronged it, right? Right? Sure, attaboy.

(As DAVID stands, wanting to move away.)

We can talk this over. We can talk this over. It's what
you did.

Who the hell you think you are? You screwed it.
A yellow whore. Some yellow ass. You put in your prick
and humped your ass. You screwed some yellow fucking
whore!

HARRIET. That's right. That's right. You were lonely and young and away from home for the very first time in your life, no white girls anywhere around –

DAVID. *(As if telling a secret.)* She was the color of the earth! They are the color of the earth, and what is white but winter with the earth under it like a suicide!

> *(As they stare at him.)*

Tell me! Tell me! Why didn't you tell me what I was?

> **(HARRIET** *throws up on the floor, maybe onto* **DAVID***'s robe, her hands at her mouth… They stand startled.)*

OZZIE. Why…don't…you ask her to cook something for you, David, will you? Make her feel better. Okay?

DAVID. I think…some eggs might be good, Mom.

OZZIE. Hear that, Harriet? David wants some eggs.

> *(Dashing off to the kitchen for a towel.)*

HARRIET. I'm all right.

> *(Laughing, almost giddy.)*

OZZIE. Of course you are. We all are.

> *(He offers his clean, white handkerchief.)*

Here, here, wipe your mouth; you've got a little something – On the corner; left side. That's it. Whata you say, David?

HARRIET. What's your pleasure, David?

DAVID. Scrambled eggs.

OZZIE. There you go. Your specialty, his pleasure.

> **(HARRIET** *darts for the kitchen, and* **OZZIE** *produces a pack of cigarettes.)*

How about a cigarette, Dave? I think I'll have one. Filter, see, brand-new idea; I tried 'em, I switched after one puff. Just a little after you left, and I just find them a lot smoother, actually; I wondered if you'd notice the new smell.

(His voice and manner growing confident.)

OZZIE. *(Cont.)* The filter's granulated. It's an off-product of corn husks. Nothing like a good smoke. Isn't that one hell of a good tasting cigarette? Isn't that one beautiful goddamn cigarette? I feel like I'm on a ship at sea.

> *(HARRIET enters with two bowls. One has a half grapefruit; the second has eggs with a spoon sticking out. She hands DAVID the grapefruit.)*

HARRIET. Here's a little grapefruit to tide you over till I get the eggs.

> *(Stirring the eggs, in preparation of scrambling them.)*

Won't be long, I promise – but I was just wondering wouldn't it be nice if we could all go to church tonight. All together and we could make a little visit in thanksgiving of your coming home. I wouldn't ask that it be long – just –

> *(DAVID puts the cigarette out in the grapefruit and drops both onto the floor.)*

– I mean, we could go to whatever saint you wanted, it wouldn't…matter…

> *(Watching DAVID walk toward the stairs.)*

Just in…just out…

> *(As DAVID climbs the stairs.)*

OZZIE. Tired… Dave?

> *(They watch him pausing at the landing.)*

Where are you going? Bathroom?

> *(DAVID enters his room, shutting the door. HARRIET heads for the phone.)*

Harriet, what's up?

HARRIET. I'm calling Father Donald.

OZZIE. Father Donald?

HARRIET. We need help, I'm calling for help.

OZZIE. Now wait a minute. No. Oh, no, no we –

HARRIET. Do you still refuse to see it? He was involved with one of them. You know what the Bible says about those people. You heard him. You heard what he said.

OZZIE. Just not Father Donald; please, please. That's all I ask – just –

> (**HARRIET** *shushes him and turns her back, waiting for someone to answer the phone.*)

Why must everything be turned into a matter of personal vengeance?

> (*And the door pops open and in comes bounding* **RICK**, *guitar upon his back.*)

RICK. *(Very cheery.)* Hi, Mom, hi, Dad.

HARRIET. *(Cheery.)* Hi, Rick!

RICK. Hi, Mom.

OZZIE. *(Cheery.)* Hi, Rick.

RICK. *(Cheery.)* Hi, Dad.

OZZIE. How you doin', Rick?

RICK. Fine, Dad. You?

OZZIE. Fine.

RICK. Good.

HARRIET. I'll get you some fudge in just a minute, Ricky!

RICK. Okay. How's Dave doin', Dad?

> (*Fiddling with his camera.*)

OZZIE. Dave's doin' fine, Rick.

RICK. Boy, I'm glad to hear that. I'm really glad to hear that, because, boy, I'll sure be glad when everything's back to the regular way. Dave's too serious, Dad; don't you think so? That's what I think. Whata you think, Dad?

> (*He snaps a picture of* **OZZIE**, *who is posing.* **RICK** *sits on the couch looking at a comic.* **OZZIE** *is seated at the other end of the couch.*)

HARRIET. Shhhhhhh! Everybody!

> *(Back to the phone.)*

Yes, yes. Oh, Father, I didn't recognize your voice. No, I don't know who. Well, yes, it's about my son, Father, David. Yes.

Well, I don't know if you know it or not, but he just got back from the war and he's troubled.

Deeply. Yes.

> *(As she listens,* **RICK** *snaps a picture of her. She tries to wave him away.)*

Deeply.

> *(Pacing with the phone and its long cord behind them.)*

Deeply, yes. Oh. So do you think you might be able to stop over sometime soon to talk to him or not? Father, any time that would be convenient for you. Yes. Oh, that would be wonderful. Yes. Oh, thank you. And may God reward *you*, Father.

> *(Hanging up the phone, she stands a moment, sort of daydreaming.)*

OZZIE. *(On the couch.)* I say to myself, "What does it mean that he is my son? How the hell is it that…he…is my son?" I mean, they say something of you joined to something of me and became…him…but what kinda goddamn explanation is that? One mystery taking the place of another? Mystery doesn't explain mystery!

RICK. *(Scarcely looking up from his comic.)* Mom, hey, c'mon, how about that fudge?

HARRIET. Ricky, oh, I'm sorry. I forgot.

> *(Hurrying into the kitchen.)*

OZZIE. And they've got…diseases…!

HARRIET. What…?

OZZIE. Dirty, filthy diseases. They got 'em. Those girls. Infection. From the blood of their parents it goes right into the fluids of their bodies. Malaria, TB. An actual rot alive in them… Gonorrhea, syphilis. There are some who have the plague. He touched them. It's disgusting.

RICK. Mom, I'm starving, honest to God; and I'm thirsty, too.

HARRIET. Yes, of course. Oh, oh.

RICK. And bring a piece for Dad, too; Dad looks hungry.

OZZIE. No.

RICK. Sure, a big sweet chocolate piece o' fudge.

OZZIE. No. Please. I don't feel well.

RICK. It'll do you good.

HARRIET. *(Entering with a tray of two servings of fudge and milk.)* Ricky, here, come here.

(Pointing him to the table.)

RICK. *(Hurrying toward her.)* What?

HARRIET. *(Handing him fudge and milk.)* Look good?

OZZIE. Or maybe we're just – I mean, maybe – Maybe it's just that he's growing away from us, like he's supposed to – like we did ourselves, from our own parents, only we thought it would happen in some other way, some –

HARRIET. *(Putting fudge and milk down on the coffee table in front of **OZZIE**.)* What are you talking about, "going away"? – He's right upstairs.

OZZIE. I don't want that.

HARRIET. You said you did.

OZZIE. He said he did.

*(**HARRIET** indicates to **RICK** that she wants to go to church, maybe with a little signal like a blessing.)*

RICK. *(Having gobbled the fudge and milk.)* You want me to drive you, Mom?

HARRIET. Would you, Ricky, please?

RICK. *(Running.)* I'll go around and get the car.

HARRIET. It's all cut and poured. Ozzie, it'll just be a waste.

OZZIE. I don't care – I don't want it.

HARRIET. You're so childish. Honest to God, you're like a two-year-old sometimes.

>   *(Heading for the door to go out.)*

OZZIE. Don't you know I could throw you down onto this floor and make another child live inside you now!

HARRIET. I doubt that, Ozzie.

OZZIE. You want me to do it?

HARRIET. *(Going out the door.)* Oh, Ozzie, Ozzie, don't we have enough trouble?

>   *(She shuts the door and he is alone. He eyes the audience.)*

OZZIE. They think they know me and they know nothing. They don't know how I feel. How I'd like to beat Ricky with my fists till his face is ugly! How I'd like to throw David out on the streets. How I'd like to cut her tongue from her mouth! They know nothing…! I was myself.

>   *(It's clear the audience is his friend.)*

I lived in a time beyond anything they can ever know – a time beyond and separate, and I was nobody's goddamn father and nobody's goddamn husband! I was myself! And I could run. I got a scrapbook of victories; a bag of medals and ribbons. Nobody was faster. In the town in which I lived my name was spoken in the factories and in the fields all around because I was the best there was. I beat the finest anybody had to offer. Summers… I would sit out on this old wood porch on the front of our house and my strength was in me, quiet and mine. Around the corner would come some old Model T Ford and scampering up the walk this bone-stiff, buck-toothed old farmer raw as Winter and cawing at me like a crow: they had one for me. Out at the edge of town. A runner from another county. My shoes are in a brown paper bag at my feet and I snatch it up and set out into the dusk, easy as breathing. There's an old white fence where we start and we run for the sun. For a hundred yards or a thousand yards or a thousand thousand. It doesn't matter. Whatever they want. I run the race they think their specialty and I beat them. They sweat and struggle, I simply glide on one step beyond…no matter what their effort, and the sun bleeds before me… We cross rivers and deserts; we clamber over mountains. I run the races the farmers arrange and I win the bets they make; and then, a few days after, the race money comes to me anonymously in the mail; but it's not for the money that I run. In the fields and factories, they speak my name when they sit down to their lunches. If there's a prize to be run for, it's me they send for. It's to be the one-sent-for that I run.

DAVID. *(Lying in bed on his back.)* And then…you left.

OZZIE. What?

DAVID. I said… "And then you left." That town.

OZZIE. Left?

DAVID. Yes. Went away; traveled. Left it all behind.

OZZIE. No. What do you mean?

DAVID. I mean, you're no longer there; you're here now.

OZZIE. But I didn't really leave it. I mean, not leave. Not really.

DAVID. Of course you did. Where are you?

OZZIE. That's not the point, Dave. Where I am isn't the point at all.

DAVID. But it is. It's everything; all that other is gone.

(As OZZIE starts for the door.)

Where are you going?

OZZIE. Groceries. Gotta go get groceries. You want anything at the grocery store?

(Looks at his watch.)

It's late. I gotta get busy.

(Rushing out the door.)

DAVID. That's all right, Dad. I'll see you later.
  (Blackout. Music.)

Scene Four

(Lights up. **RICK** *enters the living room, toying with his guitar, plinking a note or two, as* **HARRIET** *emerges from the kitchen, carrying a tray with drinks, glasses, a pot of coffee, cups, and a bowl of chips on it as* **OZZIE** *appears upstairs, coming down the hall, carrying an 8-mm movie projector already loaded with film and a folded up screen, which he sets beside the stairs.)*

HARRIET. Tune her up now, Rick.

OZZIE. What's the movie about, anyway?

HARRIET. It's probably scenery, don't you think? – Trees and fields and those little ponds. Everything over there's so green and lovely. Enough chips, Ricky?

RICK. Are we gonna have pretzels, too? 'Cause if there's both pretzels and chips then there's enough chips.

HARRIET. Ozzie.

(They scurry about with their preparations.)

OZZIE. David shoot it, or somebody else…? Anybody know? I tried to peek – put a couple feet up to the light…

(Setting up the projector on a TV tray.)

HARRIET. What did you see?

OZZIE. Nothing. Couldn't see a thing.

HARRIET. Well, I'll just bet there's one of those lovely little ponds in it somewhere.

OZZIE. *(Bent over, running a cord from the projector to the wall plug.)* Harriet, do you know when David was talking about that trouble in Hank's hand being congenital, what did you think? You think it's possible? I don't myself. I mean, we knew Hank well. I think it's just something David got mixed up about and nobody corrected him. What do you think? Is that what you think?

(As **HARRIET** *sees* **DAVID** *out of his room at the top of the stairs about to come down, she tries to warn* **OZZIE** *of* **DAVID***'s presence.)*

HARRIET. Ozzie.

OZZIE. Whatsamatter?

(Stopping, startled as he sees she is signaling him. Looking up the stairs behind him, he sees **DAVID**, *preparing to descend. He wears a tie.)*

Oh.

HARRIET. Hello!

OZZIE. Oh. Hey, oh, let me give you a hand. Yes. Yes. You look good. Good to see you.

(On the move to **DAVID** *to help him down the stairs to the big armchair.)*

Yes, sir. I think, all things considered, I think we can figure we're over the hump now and it's all downhill and good from here on in. I mean, we've talked things over, Dave, what do you say? The air's been cleared, that's what I mean – the wounds acknowledged, the healing begun. It's the ones that aren't acknowledged – the ones that aren't talked over they're the ones that do the deep damage. That's always what happens.

HARRIET. I've baked a cake, David. Happy, happy being home.

OZZIE. And we've got pop and ice and chips, and Rick is going to sing some songs.

HARRIET. Maybe we can all sing along if we want.

RICK. Anything special you'd like to hear, Dave?

OZZIE. You just sing what you know, Rick; sing what you care for, and you'll do it best.

(As he and **HARRIET** *settle down on the couch, all smiles.)*

RICK. How about "Baby, When I Find You"?

HARRIET. Ohhh, that's such a good one.

RICK. Dave, you just listen to me go! I'm gonna shake it up and build!

>   *(Rendering an excited lead into the song.)*

I'm gonna build, build, build.

>   *(And he sings.)*

BABY, WHEN I FIND YOU,
NEVER, GONNA STAND BEHIND YOU, GONNA, GONNA LEAD
    YOU
SOFTLY AT THE START,
GENTLY BY THE HEART, SWEET... LOVE...!
SLIPPING SOFTLY TO THE SEA, YOU AND ME BOTH MINE
    WONDROUS AS A GREEN
GROWING FOREST VINE...
BABY, WHEN I FIND YOU,
NEVER, GONNA STAND BEHIND YOU, GONNA, GONNA LEAD
    YOU
SOFTLY AT THE START,
GENTLY BY THE HEART, SWEET... LOVE...!
BABY, WHEN I FIND YOU.

>   *(Both he and **HARRIET** clap and laugh.)*

OZZIE. Ohhh, great, Rick, great, you burn me up with envy, honest to God.

HARRIET. It was just so wonderful. Oh, thank you so much.

RICK. I just love to do it so much, you know?

OZZIE. Has he got something goin' for him, Dave? Huh? Hey! You don't even have a drink. Take this one; take mine!

>   *(They hurry back and forth from **DAVID** to the table.)*

HARRIET. And here's some cake.

OZZIE. How 'bout some pretzels, Dave?

RICK. Tell me what you'd like to hear.

DAVID. I'd like to sing.

>   *(They stare at **DAVID**.)*

RICK. What?

OZZIE. What's that?

DAVID. I have something I'd like to sing.

RICK. Dave, you don't sing.

>   *(Strumming away.)*

DAVID. *(Reaching at the air.)* I'd like to use the guitar, if I could.

HARRIET. What are you saying?

OZZIE. C'mon, you couldn't carry a tune in a bucket and you know it. Rick's the singer, Rick and your mom. C'mon now, Rick, let's go! That can't be all we're gonna hear.

>   **(ZUNG** *is coming down the stairs now, seemingly from the attic.)*

DAVID. You're so selfish, Rick; your hair is black; it glistens. You smile. You sing. People think you are the songs you sing. They never see you. Give me the guitar.

>   *(And he clamps his hand on the guitar, stopping the music.)*

RICK. Mom, what's wrong with Dave?

DAVID. Give it to me.

RICK. Listen, you eat your cake and drink your drink and if you still wanna, I'll let you.

DAVID. Now!

HARRIET. Ozzie, make David behave.

OZZIE. Don't you play too roughly…

DAVID. Ricky…!

RICK. I don't think he's playing, Dad.

OZZIE. You watch out what you're doing…

>   **(DAVID** *grabs at the guitar.)*

RICK. You got cake all over your fingers, you'll get it all sticky, the strings all sticky –

>   *(Struggling to keep his guitar.)*

RICK Just tell me what you want to hear, I'll do it for you!

HARRIET. What is it? What's wrong?

DAVID. Give me. Give me now!

> (**DAVID** *wrenches the guitar from* **RICK**'s *hands, sending* **RICK** *sprawling.*)

OZZIE. David, dammit now.

HARRIET. Ohhhh, no, no, you're ruining everything. What's wrong with you?

OZZIE. I thought we were gonna have a nice party –

DAVID. We are!

OZZIE. No, no, I mean a nice party – One where everybody's happy.

DAVID. I'm happy. I'm singing. Don't you see them? Don't you see them?

OZZIE. Pardon, Dave?

HARRIET. What…are you saying?

DAVID. I have home movies. I thought you knew.

HARRIET. Well…we do.

OZZIE. Movies?

DAVID. Yes, I took them.

RICK. I thought you wanted to sing.

OZZIE. I mean, they're what's planned, Dave. That's what's up. The projector's all wound and ready. I don't know what you had to get so worked up for.

HARRIET. Somebody set up the screen.

OZZIE. Sure, sure. No need for all that yelling.

DAVID. I'll narrate.

OZZIE. Fine, sure. What's it about, anyway?

HARRIET. Are you in it?

OZZIE. Ricky, set up the screen. C'mon, c'mon.

DAVID. It's a kind of story.

RICK. What about my guitar?

(**RICK** *tries for the guitar as he passes on his way to open and stand the screen facing front, upstage of the couch.*)

DAVID. No.

(*Keeping it.*)

OZZIE. We oughta have some popcorn, though.

HARRIET. Oh, yes, what a dumb movie house, no popcorn, huh, Rick!

RICK. Pretty dumb, Dad.

OZZIE. Let her rip, Dave.

(*Switching off the lights.*)

Ready when you are, C.B.

HARRIET. Shhhhhh!

(**DAVID** *turns on the projector;* **OZZIE** *is hurrying back to the couch for a seat.* **ZUNG** *has sat down in the middle of the couch,* **HARRIET** *on one side,* **OZZIE** *on the other.*)

OZZIE. Let her rip, Cecile B… I want a new contract, Cecile B.

(**OZZIE** *and* **HARRIET** *angle upstage to watch. The projector runs, the screen blank except for a greenish glare, and the flickering of the light.*)

HARRIET. Ohhh, what's the matter? It didn't come out, there's nothing there.

DAVID. Of course there is.

HARRIET. Noooo… It's all funny.

DAVID. Look.

OZZIE. It's underexposed, Dave.

DAVID. No. Look.

HARRIET. What?

DAVID. They hang in the trees. They hang by their wrists half-severed by the wire.

OZZIE. Pardon me, Dave?

HARRIET. I'm going to put on the lights.

DAVID. Noooo! Look! They hang in the greenish haze eaten by insects; a woman and a man, middle-aged, they don't shout or cry. He's too small.

Look: he seems all bone, shame in his eyes that his wife has come even here with him, skinny also as a broom and her hair straight and black, hanging to mask her eyes.

OZZIE. I don't know what you're doing, David; there's nothing up there. I mean, it just didn't – come out.

DAVID. Look.

> (**DAVID** *moves near the screen.*)

They are all bone and pain, uncontoured and ugly but for the peculiar melon swelling in her middle which is her pregnancy – which they do not see – Look! These soldiers who have found her, as they do not see that she is not dead but only dying until saliva and blood bubble at her lips.

> (*He steps in front of the screen and looks out into the projector light which washes over him, over* **ZUNG** *and* **OZZIE** *and* **HARRIET**, *his shadow on the screen.*)

Look…! And yet she dies. Though a doctor is called in to remove the bullet-shot baby she would have preferred to keep since she was dying and it was dead. In fact, as it turned out they would have all been better off left to hang as they had been strung on the wires – he with the back of his head blown off and she – the rifle jammed exactly and deeply up into her and a bullet fired directly into the child living there. For they ended each buried in a separate place; the husband by chance alone was returned to their village, while the wife was dumped into a random plot of dirt, while the child, too small a piece of meat, was burned. Thrown into fire as the shattered legs and arms cut off of men are burned. There is an oven. It's not a ceremony. It's the disposal of garbage…!

*(HARRIET marches to the projector, pulls the plug.
ZUNG rises and climbs the stairs until she is out
of sight.)*

HARRIET. It's so awful the things those yellow people do
to one another. Yellow people hanging yellow people.
Isn't that right? Ozzie, I told you – animals – Christ
burn them.

*(She returns the guitar to RICK, helps DAVID to sit
on the couch.)*

David, don't let it hurt you. All the things you saw.
People aren't themselves in war. I mean like that sticking
that gun into that poor woman and then shooting that
poor little baby, that's not human. That's inhuman. It's
inhuman, barbaric and uncivilized and inhuman. It's
inhuman. It's inhuman and barbaric and uncivilized.

DAVID. I'm thirsty.

HARRIET. For what? Tell me. Water? Or would you like
some milk? How about some milk?

DAVID. No.

HARRIET. Or would you like some orange juice? All golden
and little bits of ice.

DAVID. Coffee.

HARRIET. Coffee. Cream only, right? No sugar.

(As she prepares the coffee for him.)

OZZIE. Just all those words and that film with no picture
and these poor people hanging somewhere so you can
bring them home like this house is a meat house – what
do you think you're doing?

HARRIET. Oh, Ozzie, no, it's not that – No – He's just
young, a young boy and he's been through terrible
terrible things and now he's home, with his family he
loves, just trying to speak to those he loves – just –

DAVID. Yes!

*(Helping her finish her thought, excited by this
amazing new idea, waving his cane, knocking
party things around.)*

That's right; yes. What I mean is, yes, of course. That's what I am.

(The cane almost hits **OZZIE**, *knocking glasses, soda cans, knick knacks aside, as* **HARRIET** *scurries about, trying to catch these items before they break. The cane is pointed at* **OZZIE**.*)*

A young...blind man in a room...in a house in the dark, raising nothing in a gesture of no meaning toward two voices who are not speaking of a certain...incredible... connection!

RICK. Listen, everybody, I hate to rush off like this, but I gotta. Night.

*(***RICK*** runs for the stairs, taking his guitar, some pop and chips with him.)*

HARRIET. Good night, Rick. Good night.

OZZIE. Good night.

DAVID. Because I talk of certain things...don't think I did them. Murderers don't even know that murder happens.

HARRIET. What are you saying? No, no. We're family, that's all – we've had a little trouble – No need to talk of murder, David, you've got to stop – please – no more yelling. Just be happy and home like all the others – why can't you?

DAVID. You mean take some old man to a ditch of water, shove his head under, and talk of cars and money till his feeble pawing stops and then head on home to go in and out of doors and drive cars.

(Beat.)

I left her where people are thin and small all their lives.

(Another realization.)

Or did you think it was a place...like this? Sinks and kitchens all the world over? Is that what you believe? Water from faucets, light from wires? Trucks, telephones, TV. Ricky sings and sings, but if I were to cut his throat, he would no longer and you would miss him – you would miss him singing.

(Wearily turning to go.)

We're hoboes! We make...signs...in the dark. You know yours. I understand my own. We share...coffee!

(Climbing the stairs.)

I'm going up to bed...now. I'm very, very...tired.

OZZIE. Well...you have a good sleep, son...

DAVID. Yes, I think I'll sleep in.

(ZUNG, who waits at the top of the stairs, follows him up into his room.)

OZZIE. You do as you please...

DAVID. Good night.

HARRIET. Good night.

OZZIE. Good night.

HARRIET. Good night.

(Slight pause.)

You get a good rest. Try...

(Silence; they stand and then start to clean up the scattered plates, glasses, chips, the projector, tray table, screen.)

I'm...hungry... Ozzie... Are you hungry?

OZZIE. Hungry...?

HARRIET. Yes.

OZZIE. No. Oh, no.

(As they go in and out of the kitchen.)

HARRIET. How do you feel? You look a little peaked. Do you feel all right?

OZZIE. I'm fine; I'm fine.

HARRIET. You look funny.

OZZIE. Really. No. How about yourself?

HARRIET. I'm never sick; you know that. Just a little sleepy.

OZZIE. Well, that's no wonder. It's been a long day.

HARRIET. Yes, it has.

OZZIE. No wonder.

HARRIET. Good night

OZZIE. Good night.

HARRIET. Don't stay up too late now.

OZZIE. Do you know when he was waving that cane and he pointed it at me? I couldn't breathe. I felt for an instant that I might never breathe.

> (**HARRIET**, *with a tray of dishes, starts for the kitchen.*)

HARRIET. Mmmmmmmm. Ohhh, I'm so sleepy. I'm sooo sleepy. Aren't you sleepy?

OZZIE. Harriet! I couldn't breathe.

HARRIET. What do you want? Teaching him sports and fighting?

> (*Rage shattering her motherly control.*)

WHAT... OZZIE... DO YOU WANT?

OZZIE. Well... I was wondering... Do we have any aspirin down here... Or are they all upstairs?

HARRIET. I thought you said you felt well.

OZZIE. Well, I do. It's just a tiny headache. Hardly worth mentioning.

HARRIET. There's aspirin in the cabinet.

OZZIE. (*Crossing.*) Which side?

HARRIET. Right-hand side.

OZZIE. Get me a glass of water, would you, please?

HARRIET. Of course.

> (*Hurrying into the kitchen.*)

OZZIE. Thank you. It's not much of a headache, actually. Actually it's just a tiny headache.

> (*He pops the pill into his mouth and drinks to wash it down.*)

HARRIET. Aspirin makes your stomach bleed. Did you know that? Nobody knows why. It's part of how it works. It just does it; makes you bleed. This extremely tiny series of hemorrhages in those delicate inner tissues. It's like those thin membranes begin, in a very minor way to sweat blood and you bleed; inside yourself you bleed.

(Turning, she crosses away.)

OZZIE. That's not true. None of that. You made all that up. Where are you going?

(As she puts a coat on from the coat rack, goes out the door.)

I mean, are you going out? Where…are you off to?

(The door is closed and she's gone.)

Goddammit, there's something going on around here; don't you want to know what it is? I want to know what it is.

(Marching to the phone, dialing for the operator.)

I want to know what's going on around here. I want to – I got to.

(As the operator answers.)

Get me the police. That's right, goddammit – I want somebody – I want one of you people to get on out to 717 Dunbar and do some checking, some checking at 717 – What? Ohhh –

(Whispering.)

Christ…! Just a second, I gotta be –

(Pulling a handkerchief from his pocket, he covers the mouthpiece.)

I mean, they got a kid living there who just got back from the war and he's carrying a very heavy duffle bag and something's going on and I want to know what it is. No, I don't wanna give my name. It's them, not me – they're the ones who are acting strange! They're acting very goddamn strange, the whole lot of them. It doesn't matter who I am! It only –

(Freezing, as it seems they've hung up.)

OZZIE Hey! Hey! Hey!

*(**RICK** is in the upstairs hall, headed down, guitar over his shoulder, with his camera as always.)*

RICK. *(So very cheery.)* Hey, Dad! How you doin'?

OZZIE. *(Cheery.)* Oh, Rick! Hi!

RICK. Hi! How you doin'?

(Heading toward the door.)

OZZIE. Fine. Just fine.

RICK. Good.

OZZIE. How you doin', Rick?

RICK. Well, I'll see you later.

OZZIE. I want you to teach me the guitar!

RICK. What?

OZZIE. I want you to teach me…guitar…! To play it.

(Pulling up chairs to the table for them to sit.)

RICK. Sure. Okay.

(Taking a seat with his guitar.)

OZZIE. I want to learn to play it. They've always been a kind of mystery to me, pianos…guitars.

RICK. Mystery?

OZZIE. I mean, what do you think? Do you ever have to think what your fingers should be doing? What I mean is do you ever have to say – I don't know what – "This finger goes there and this other one does –" I mean, "It's on this ridge, now I chord all the strings and then switch it all." See? And do you have to tell yourself, "Now switch it all – first finger this ridge – second finger, down – third – somewhere." I mean, does that kind of thing ever happen? I mean, how do you play it? I keep having this notion of wanting some…thing…some material thing, and I've built it. And then there's this feeling I'm of value, that I'm on my way – I mean, moving – and I'm going to come to something eventually, some kind of achievement. All these feelings of a child...in me...they shoot through me and then they're gone and they're not anything anymore. But it's a...wall that I want... I think. I see myself doing it sometimes. All brick and stone. Coils of steel. And then I finish...and the success of it is monumental and people come from far. To see... To look. They applaud. Ricky...teach me.

RICK. Ahhh...what, Dad?

OZZIE. Guitar, guitar.

RICK. Oh; sure. Great. First you start with the basic "C" chord. You put the first finger on the second string.

OZZIE. But that's what I'm talking about. You don't do that. I know you don't.

RICK. *(Thinking he has misunderstood.)* Oh.

OZZIE. You just pick it up and play it. I don't have time for all that you're saying. That's what I've been telling you.

RICK. Well, maybe some other day then.

> *(On his way for the door.)*

OZZIE. What?

RICK. Maybe Mom'll wanna learn, too.

OZZIE. No, no.

RICK. Just me and you then.

OZZIE. Right. Me and you.

RICK. I'll see you later.

OZZIE. What? Where are you going?

RICK. Maybe tomorrow we can do it.

OZZIE. No.

RICK. Well, maybe the next day then.

> *(And the door shuts.)*

OZZIE. No, now, now!

(Beat; he is alone. He looks into the audience, explaining.)

OZZIE I grew too old too quick. It was just a town I thought and no one remained to test me. I didn't even know it was leaving I was doing. I thought I'd go away and come back. Not leave.

(Looking up at DAVID's room.)

You son of a bitch.

(Running up to DAVID's room.)

Not leave!

(Entering DAVID's room.)

Restless, Dave; restless. Got a lot on my mind. Some of us can't just lay around, you know. You said I left that town like I was wrong, but I was right. A man proved himself by leaving, by going out into the world; he tested himself. So I went and then I ended up in the goddamn Depression, what about that? I stood in goddamn lines of people begging bread and soup. You're not the only one who's had troubles. All of us, by God, David, think about that a little. Just give somebody besides yourself some goddamn thought for a change.

(Stepping out the door, slamming it. He turns to the audience, his friends.)

I'm expecting I'll step into the best part of my life and I walk right into the Depression.

(Coming down the stairs back into the living room.)

I lived in goddamn dirty fields with thousands of other men. Baffled. Wondering what hit us. We made tents of our coats. Traveled on freight trains. Again and again... the whole of the length of this country, soot in my fingers, riding the rails. A bum, a hobo, but young. And then one day...there's a brakeman – this brakeman, who sees me hunched down in that railroad cattle car and he orders me off. He stands distant, ordering that I jump…! I don't understand, and then he stops speaking…and…when he speaks again, there's pain is in his eyes and voice – "You're a runner," he says, "Christ, I didn't know you were a runner." Somehow he knows me. And he moves to embrace me, and with both hands he takes me and lifts me far out and I fall, I roll. All in the air, then slam down breathless, raw from the cinders…bruised and dizzy at the outskirts of this town. And I'm here, I'm gone from that other town. I'm here.

(He looks around the house where he lives.)

Here. I make friends. We have good times even though things are rough. We point young girls out on the street. I start thinking about them; I start having dreams of horses and breasts and crotches. And then one day the feeling is in me that I must see a train go by and I'll get on it or I won't, something will happen, but halfway down to where I was thrown off, I see how the grass growing in among the ties is tall, the rails rusted. Grass grows in abundance. Trains no longer come that way; they all go some other way…and far behind me, I turn to see Harriet, young and lovely, weaving among the weeds. I feel the wonder of her body moving toward me. She's the thing I'll enter to find my future, I think.

(Slowly lowering to the couch.)

Yes. It's her. "Yes," I yell. "Sonofabitch! Bring her here! C'mon! Bring her on! It's my life! I can do it!" Swollen with pride, screaming and yelling, I stand there: "I'm ready. I'm ready… I'm ready."

(As he has sunk down onto the couch, as if falling asleep. Lights hold him in a small socket, as everything else goes black.)

Scene Five

(As **OZZIE** *sleeps on the couch, the closet door in* **DAVID***'s room opens in the dark and* **ZUNG** *enters.* **DAVID** *startles and sits up abruptly.)*

DAVID. What? What?

(Lights come up now on the living room and in **DAVID***'s room, bringing daylight. Still* **OZZIE** *sleeps on the couch.)*

Who's there?

(Standing.)

There's someone there? Who's there?

(Sensing **ZUNG,** **DAVID** *stops and stands at attention, as* **RICK** *comes in from the kitchen with a plate of several sandwiches and a bottle of pop as* **HARRIET** *appears on an upstairs hallway...)*

HARRIET. *(Calling down to* **RICK.***)* Hey, Rick have you seen my crossword puzzle book?

RICK. In the bathroom, Mom.

HARRIET. Bathroom...? Did I leave it there?

RICK. Guess so, Mom.

(As **HARRIET** *goes back toward the bathroom,* **RICK** *heads toward the kitchen table intending to sit, eat, and read his comic.)*

*(***DAVID***, moving into the hall, where he searches the air with his cane, bumps into something.* **RICK** *turns and sees him.)*

(Hurrying over to **DAVID** *in the hall.)* Whatsamatter? Dave?

DAVID. What?

(Descending the stairs.)

RICK. It's just me and Dad and Dad's sleeping.

DAVID. Sleeping? Is he?

RICK. On the couch. You want me to wake him?

DAVID. No...no.

>   (*Moving down to the living room.*)

RICK. Hey, could I get some pictures, Dave? Would you mind?

DAVID. Of course not. No.

RICK. Let me just go get some film and some flashes, okay?
DAVID. Sure.

>   (**RICK** *dashes up the stairs.*)

OZZIE. Pardon? Par...don?

>   (*Following the sound,* **DAVID** *finds the couch and*
>   **OZZIE.** *He crouches behind the couch. In* **DAVID**'s
>   *room upstairs,* **ZUNG** *sits on the bed, facing out,*
>   *looking down at the living room.*)

DAVID. (*Whispering, leaning near.*) I think you should know I've begun to hate you. I don't think you can tell me any more. I must tell you. Does that disturb you?

>   (*As* **OZZIE** *stirs.*)

If I had been an orphan with no one to count on me, I would have stayed there.

>   (*As* **OZZIE** *stirs more.*)

Restless, are you? You think us good, and yet we steal all you have.

OZZIE. Good...ole...Hank.

DAVID. No, no.

OZZIE. Nooo...nooo...

DAVID. Her name was Zung. Zung. She would tell me you would not like her – she would touch her fingers to her eyes and nose, and she knew how I must feel sometimes just like you.

OZZIE. Ohhh, nooo... Sleeping...

DAVID. You must hear me. It is only fraud that keeps us sane. I swear it.

OZZIE. David, sleeping...! Oh, oh...

DAVID. It's not innocence I have lost! What is it I have lost?

OZZIE. Oh…oh…

*(As **RICK** comes hurrying down the stairs.)*

DAVID. Don't you know? Do you see her in your sleep? I think I do sometimes.

RICK. I meant to get some good shots at the party, but I never got a chance the way things turned out. You can stay right there.

DAVID. I'll sit, all right?

*(As **DAVID** starts, **RICK** helps him to the chair.)*

RICK. Sure. How you feelin', anyway, Dave? I mean, honest ta God, I'm hopin' you get better. Everybody is.

*(As **DAVID** settles into the recliner.)*

I mean…you're not gonna go talkin' anymore crazy like about that guitar and all that, are you? You know what I mean. Not to Mom and Dad, anyway. It scares 'em and then I get scared and I don't like it, okay?

DAVID. Sure. That guitar business wasn't serious, anyway, Rick. None of that. It was all just a little joke I felt like playing, a kind of little game.

*(As **RICK** snaps a picture.)*

I was only trying to show you how I hate you.

RICK. Huh?

DAVID. To see you die is why I live, Rick.

RICK. Oh.

*(**HARRIET** comes along the hall and down the stairs, the crossword puzzle book is in her hands.)*

HARRIET. Goodness gracious, Ricky, it was just where you said it would be, though I'm sure I don't know how it got there because I didn't put it there. Hello, David.

*(As she and **RICK** settle at the kitchen table.)*

DAVID. Hello.

OZZIE. OHHHHHHHHHHHHHHH!

> *(Screaming, he wakes up.)*

Oh, boy, What a dream! Oh…

> *(Trying to get to his feet, but falling back.)*

Ohhhhhhh! God, leg's asleep. Jesus!

> *(Flopping about, he sits there, rubbing his leg.)*

Ohhhh, everybody. Scared the hell out of me, that dream. I hollered. Did you hear me? And my leg's asleep, too.

> *(He hits the leg, stomps the floor.)*

Did anybody hear me holler?

HARRIET. *(At the table, absorbed in the crossword puzzle.)* Not me.

RICK. What did you dream about, Dad?

OZZIE. I don't remember, but it was awful.

> *(Stamping his foot.)*

Ohhhh, wake up, wake up. Hank was in it, though. And Dave. They stood over me, whispering – I could feel how they hated me.

RICK. *(Looking up from the sandwich he's eating and the comic he's reading.)* That really happened; he really did that, Dad.

OZZIE. Who did?

RICK. What you said.

OZZIE. No, no. I was sleeping. It scared me awful in my sleep. I'm still scared, honest to God, it was so awful.

DAVID. It's that sleeping in funny positions, Dad. It's that sleeping in some place that's not a bed.

OZZIE. Pardon?

DAVID. Makes you dream funny. What did Hank look like?

HARRIET. Ozzie, how do you spell "Apollo"?

OZZIE. What?

RICK. Jesus, Dad, Schroeder got three home runs, you hear about that? Two in the second of the first and one in the third of the second. Goddamn, if he don't make MVP in the National, I'll eat my socks. You hear about that, Dad?

OZZIE. Yes, I did. Yes.

RICK. He's somethin'.

OZZIE. A pro.

HARRIET. Ozzie, can you think of a four-letter word that starts with "G" and ends with "B"?

RICK. Glub.

HARRIET. Glub?

OZZIE. Glub?

RICK. Glub. It's a cartoon word. Cartoon people say it when they're drowning. G-L-U-B.

OZZIE. Ricky. Ricky, I was wondering…when I was sleeping, were my eyes open? Was I seeing?

RICK. I didn't notice, Dad.

HARRIET. "Glub" doesn't work, Rick.

RICK. Try "Grub." That's what sourdoughs call their food. It's G – R –

OZZIE. Wait a minute!

RICK. G – R –

OZZIE. All of you wait a minute! Listen! Listen. I mean, I look for explanations. I look inside myself. For an explanation. I mean, I look inside MY self. As I would look into water or the sky. The ocean. They're silver. Answers…silver and elusive…like fish. But if you can catch them in the sea…hook them as they flash by, snatch them up…drag them down like birds from the sky…against all their struggle…when you're adrift and starving…they…can help you live.

RICK. Mom… Dad's hungry… I think. He wants some fish.

OZZIE. Shut up!

RICK. *(Hurt.)* Dad…

OZZIE. Piece of shit! Shut up! Shut up!

HARRIET. Ozzie…!

OZZIE. *(Focusing on* **DAVID.***)* I don't want to hear about her. I'm not interested in her. You did what you did and I was no part of it. You understand me? I don't want to hear any more about her! Look at him. Sitting there. Listening. I'm tired of hearing you, Dave. You understand that? I'm tired of hearing you and your crybaby voice and your crybaby stories. And your crybaby slobbering and your –

> *(Glaring at* **DAVID.***)*

Look…at…him! You make me want to vomit! Harriet! You –

> *(Still sitting but connecting to* **HARRIET** *at the table behind him.)*

You! Your internal organs – your internal female organs – they've got some kind of poison in them. They're backing up some kind of rot into the world. I think you ought to have them cut out of you. I mean, I just can't stop thinking about it. I just can't stop thinking about it. Little bitty chinky kids you wanted to have. Little bitty chinky yellow kids. Didn't you. For our grandchildren! Little bitty yellow puffy…creatures…! For our grandchildren! That's all you cared!

HARRIET. Ohhh, Ozzie, God forgive you the cruelty of your words. All children are God's children.

> *(***DAVID** *stands up, looking up at his room where* **ZUNG** *sits on the bed in changing light. He runs to the stairs and up to her.)*

DAVID. *(Coming in the door, seeing her.)* I didn't know you were here. I didn't know. I'll buy you clothing. I've lived with them all my life.

> *(Moving to her, sitting down on the bed beside her.)*

I'll make them not hate you. I'll buy you books. They will see you. The seasons will amaze you. Texas is enormous. Ohio is sometimes green. There will be time. We will learn to speak. And it will be as it was in that moment when we looked in the dark and our eyes were tongues that could speak and the hurting...all of it ...stopped, and there was total understanding in you of me and in me of you and...such delight in your eyes that I felt it.

> (**OZZIE**, *following* **DAVID**'s *movements, has climbed the stairs and he stands on the landing looking in the open door of* **DAVID**'s *room.* **ZUNG** *stands and starts to move out of the room.*)

Yet. I...discarded you. I discarded you. Forgive me.

> (*Moving after her.*)

You moved to leave as if you were struggling not to move, not leave.

> (*To* **OZZIE** *on the landing.*)

"She's the thing most possibly of value in my life," I said. "She is garbage and filth and I must get her back if I wish to live. Sickness, I must cherish her."

> (**ZUNG** *continues down the stairs and he bolts after her, pursuing her until they are by the front door.*)

Zung, there were old voices inside me I had trusted all my life as if they were my own. I didn't know I shouldn't hear them. So reasonable and calm they seemed a source of wisdom. "She's all of everything impossible made possible, cast her down," they said. And I did as they told; I did it, and now I know that I am not awake but asleep, and in my sleep...there is nothing... nothing...! What do you want from me to make you stay? I'll do it; I'll do what you want!

RICK. Lookee here, Dad.

> (**RICK** *aims his camera from the table at* **OZZIE** *who has come down, still following* **DAVID**. **OZZIE** *stands near the couch, having watched* **DAVID**... **RICK** *takes a picture. Flash.*)

(*ZUNG reaches and opens the door to go.*)

DAVID. No. Stay!

(*DAVID slams the door shut, keeping ZUNG inside and enfolding her in his arms, kissing her as OZZIE watches.*)

(*Slowly, OZZIE sits, looking out.*)

OZZIE. Glub... Glub. Glub.

(*Blackout.*)

End of Act One

ACT TWO

*(Lights up. Sunny late morning. **OZZIE** and **HARRIET** sit on the couch. **FATHER DONALD**, holding a rolled-up magazine, is seated in the recliner. **DAVID** is in his room on his bed with **ZUNG** beside him. There is a tray with tea and teacups on the coffee table. **FATHER DONALD** seems to have been talking a bit.)*

FATHER DONALD. I deal with people and their uneasiness on a regular basis, all the time, you see. Everybody I talk to is nervous…one way or another, so I anticipate no real trouble in dealing with Dave. You have no idea the things people do and then tell me once that confessional door is shut. I'm looking forward, actually, to speaking with him. Religion has been sloughed off a lot lately, but I think there's a relevancy much larger than the credit most give.

We're growing – and our insights, when we have them, are twofold. I for one have come recently to understand how very often what seems a spiritual problem is in fact a problem of the mind rather than the spirit – not that the two can in fact be separated, though, in theory, they very often are. So what we must do is apply these theories to fact. At which point we would find that mind and spirit are one and I, a priest, am a psychiatrist, and psychiatrists are priests. I mean – I feel like I'm rambling – Am I rambling?

HARRIET. Oh, no, Father.

OZZIE. Nooo…noo.

HARRIET. Father, this is hard for me to say, but I…feel…his problem is he sinned against the Sixth Commandment with whores.

FATHER DONALD. That's very likely over there.

HARRIET. And then the threat of death each day made it so much worse.

FATHER DONALD. I got the impression from our earlier talk he'd had a relationship of some duration.

HARRIET. A day or two, wouldn't you say, Ozzie?

OZZIE. *(Distracted, oddly preoccupied with his eye on the recliner where* **FATHER DONALD** *sits.)* A three-day pass I'd say. Though I don't know, of course.

FATHER DONALD. They're doing a lot of psychiatric studies on that phenomenon right now, did you know that?

> *(The front door pops open, and in bounds* **RICK** *headed straight for the kitchen.)*

HARRIET. *(Happy to see him.)* Oh, Rick!

RICK. *(Cheery.)* Hi, Mom; hi, Dad.

OZZIE. *(Cheery.)* Hi, Rick.

FATHER DONALD. Rick, hello!

RICK. Oh, Father Donald... Hi.

> *(Faltering but then speeding for the kitchen.)*

OZZIE. Look at him heading for the fudge.

FATHER DONALD. Well, he's a good big strong sturdy boy.

RICK. Hungry and thirsty.

> *(He goes.)*

FATHER DONALD. *(Calling after* **RICK.** *)* And don't you ever feel bad about it, either!

> *(Then standing.)*

Dave's up in his room, I imagine, so maybe I'll just head on up and have my little chat. He is why I'm here, after all.

HARRIET. Fine.

> *(**FATHER DONALD** heads for the stairs.)*

OZZIE. *(Still distracted, staring at the chair in which* **FATHER DONALD** *sat.)* First door top of the stairs.

FATHER DONALD. *(Pausing on the stairs.)* And could I use the bathroom, please, before I see ole Dave? Got to see a man about a horse.

HARRIET. Oh, Father, certainly; it's just down the hall. Fifth door.

OZZIE. *(Approaching the chair.)* What's wrong with that chair?

HARRIET. *(Calling up.)* It's the blue door, Father!

OZZIE. I don't like that chair. I think it's stupid-looking.

> *(Calling to the kitchen.)*

Ricky!

> *(As* **RICK** *pops in, eating fudge.)*

Ricky, sit. Sit in that chair.

RICK. What…?

OZZIE. Go on, sit, sit.

> *(***RICK*** hurries to the chair, sits, eats.* **OZZIE** *is poking and testing the chair.)*

HARRIET. Oh, Ricky, take your father's picture, he looks so silly.

OZZIE. I just don't think that chair is any good. I just don't think it's comfortable. Father Donald looked ill at ease all the while he was sitting there.

HARRIET. Well, he had to go to the bathroom, Ozzie, what do you expect?

OZZIE. *(To* **RICK.***)* Get up. It's just not right.

> *(Taking over the chair, he sits; he fidgets.)*

Noooooo. It's just not a comfortable chair at all, I don't know why.

> *(Rising, on the move toward the couch.)*

I don't like it. How much did we pay?

> *(Sitting down on the couch.)*

HARRIET. What do you think you're doing?

OZZIE. And this couch isn't comfortable either.

HARRIET. It's a lovely couch.

OZZIE. But it isn't comfortable. Nooooo. And I'm not really sure it's lovely, either. Did we pay one hundred and fifty dollars?

HARRIET. What? Oh, more.

OZZIE. How much?

HARRIET. I don't know, I told you.

OZZIE. You don't. I don't. It's gone anyway, isn't it?

HARRIET. Ozzie, what does it matter?

OZZIE. *(Already on the move for the stairs.)* I'm going upstairs. I'll be upstairs.

HARRIET. Wait a minute.

> *(As* **OZZIE** *keeps moving.)*

I want to talk to you. I think we ought to talk.

I mean, it's nothing to worry about or anything, but you don't know about it and it's your house, you're involved – so it's just something I mention.

> *(As* **OZZIE** *returns and sits with her.)*

You're the man of the house, you ought to know. The police were here. Earlier today.

OZZIE. What? Are you sure?

HARRIET. What do you mean – am I sure? I saw them; I talked to them. The police. Two of them. Two. A big and a small – they – It was just a little bit ago; not long at all.

OZZIE. Jesus Christ.

HARRIET. Oh, I know, I know. Just out of the blue like that – it's how I felt, too. I did, I did.

OZZIE. What did they want? What did they say?

HARRIET. It was when you were gone for groceries. I mean, they thought they were supposed to be here. We wanted it, they thought.

OZZIE. No, no.

HARRIET. Somebody called them to come here. They thought it had been us. They were supposed to look through David's duffle bag, they thought.

OZZIE. They – were – what?

HARRIET. That's what I mean. That's exactly what I –

OZZIE. Look through his duffle bag? There's nothing wrong with his duffle bag!

HARRIET. Isn't it incredible? Somebody called them – they didn't know who – no name was given and it sounded muffled through a handkerchief, they said. I said, "Well, it wasn't us." I told them, "Don't you worry about us. We're all all right here." It must have been a little joke by somebody.

OZZIE. What about David?

HARRIET. David?

OZZIE. Or Ricky. Did you ask Ricky?

HARRIET. Ricky?

OZZIE. *(For emphasis.)* RICKY! RICKY!

RICK. *(Popping in from the kitchen, thinking he was called.)* What's up, Dad?

OZZIE. I don't know.

RICK. I thought you called.

OZZIE. *(To* **HARRIET**.*)* You ask him; you ask him. I think the whole thing's preposterous – absolutely –

HARRIET. Ricky, do you know anything about anybody calling the police to come here?

OZZIE. *(Moving for the stairs.)* I'm going upstairs. I'll be upstairs.

RICK. The police? Oh, no, Mom, not me.

> *(As* **HARRIET** *is turning to look after* **OZZIE**.*)*

Okay if I use the car?

HARRIET. What?

FATHER DONALD. *(Encountering* **OZZIE** *in the upstairs hallway.)* Gonna take care of old Dave right now.

OZZIE. I'm going upstairs. I'll be upstairs.

(He goes as **HARRIET** *looks up at them.)*

RICK. *(Headed for the door.)* Bye, Mom.

HARRIET. What? Oh.

(Looking after **RICK** *as the door shuts behind him.)*

Be careful!

FATHER DONALD. *(Calling down to* **HARRIET.***)* Ozzie said to tell you he was going upstairs.

HARRIET. What?

FATHER DONALD. Ozzie said to tell you he was going upstairs.

HARRIET. *(Staring at him.)* Oh, Father, I'm so glad you're here.

*(***FATHER DONALD** *nods, looks at* **DAVID***'s door.* **DAVID** *lies in bed with* **ZUNG***.)*

*(***HARRIET** *goes into the kitchen, taking the tray of tea and teacups.)*

FATHER DONALD. *(He knocks on the door.)* Dave?

*(***ZUNG** *scurries into the closet as* **FATHER DONALD** *knocks again, lightly, and then opens the door; eases in to find* **DAVID** *lying in bed.)*

Dave? It's me… Dave… Ohh, Dave, golly, you look just fine. Here I expected to see you all worn out, and there you are looking so good. It's me, Dave, Father Donald. Let me shake your hand.

*(***FATHER DONALD** *moves alongside the bed to get nearer to* **DAVID***, who doesn't offer his hand.)*

Can't see me, can you.

(Trying to help **DAVID** *shake hands.)*

There you go. Yes sir, let me tell you, I'm proud. A lot of people might tell you that, I know, but I mean it, and I'll stand behind it, if there's anything I can do for you – anything at all.

DAVID. No. I'm all right.

FATHER DONALD. And that's the amazing part of it, Dave, you are. You truly are. It's plain as day. Golly, I just don't know how to tell you how glad I am to see you in such high fine spirits. Would you like my blessing? Let me just give you my blessing and then we'll talk things over a little and –

> (**DAVID**'s *cane whips and strikes into* **FATHER DONALD**'s *raised arm.*)

Ohhhhhhhhhhhhhh!

(Wincing, retreating.) Oh, Dave; oh, watch out what you're doing!

DAVID. I know.

FATHER DONALD. No, no, I mean, you swung it in the air, you – hit me.

DAVID. Yes.

FATHER DONALD. No, no, you don't understand, you –

DAVID. I was trying to hit you, Father.

FATHER DONALD. *(Taken aback.)* What?

> (As **DAVID** *moves to sit at the bottom of the bed,* **FATHER DONALD**, *back to the wall, stares.*)

DAVID. I didn't send for you.

FATHER DONALD. I know, I know, your poor mother – your poor mother –

DAVID. I don't want you here, Father; get out!

FATHER DONALD. David.

DAVID. Get out, I'm sick of you. You've been in one goddamn corner or another of this room all my life making signs at me, whispering, wanting to splash me with water or mark me with oil – some goddamn hocus-pocus. I feel reverence for the air and the air is empty, Father. Now get the fuck out of here.

FATHER DONALD. No, no, no, no, David. No, no. I can't give that to you. You'll have to get that from somewhere else.

DAVID. I don't want anything from you.

(**DAVID** *flops back on the bed, lying on his side.*)

FATHER DONALD. I'm supposed to react now in some foolish way – I see – some foolish, foolish way that will discredit me. Isn't that right. Oh, of course it is. It's an excuse to dismiss my voice that you're seeking, an excuse for the self-destruction your anger has made you think you want, and I'm supposed to give it. I'm supposed to find all this you're doing obscene and sacrilegious instead of seeing it as the gesture of true despair that it is. You're trying to make me disappear, but it's not going to happen. No, no. No such luck, David.

(As **FATHER DONALD** *pulls a chair up near the foot of the bed, but at a safe distance, he sits.*)

I understand you, you see. Everything about you.

DAVID. Do you?

FATHER DONALD. The way you're troubled.

DAVID. I didn't know that, Father.

FATHER DONALD. You say that sarcastically – "Do you? I didn't know that." As if to imply you're so complicated I couldn't ever understand you when I already have. You see, I've been looking into a few things, David, giving some things some thought. I have in my hand a magazine – you can't see it, I know, but it's there. A psychiatric journal in which there is an article of some interest and it deals with soldiers and some of them carried on as you did and then there's some others who didn't. It's not all just a matter of hocus-pocus any longer.

DAVID. *(Turning back.)* Carried…on… Father?

FATHER DONALD. That whore. That yellow whore. You understand. You knew I was bringing the truth when I came, which is why you hit me.

DAVID. I thought you didn't even know the problem. You came in here all bubbly and jolly asking how did I feel.

FATHER DONALD. That was only a little ruse, David; a little maneuver to put you off your guard. I only did that to mislead you. That's right. Your mother gave me all the basics some weeks ago and I filled in the rest from what I know. You see, if it's a fight you want, it's what you'll get. Your soul is worth some time and sweat from me. You're valued by others, David, even if you don't value yourself.

(As **DAVID** *rises to sit at the foot of the bed* **FATHER DONALD** *gestures with his magazine.)*

It's all here – right here – in these pages. It was demonstrated beyond any possible doubt that people – soldiers – who are compelled for some reason not even they themselves understand to establish personal-sexual relationships with whores are inferior to those who don't; they're maladjusted, embittered, non-goal-oriented misfits. The sexual acceptance of another person, David, is intimate and extreme; this kind of acceptance of an alien race is in fact the rejection of one's own race – it is in fact the rejection of one's own self – it is sickness, David.

*(***DAVID*** seems to crumple under the weight of what* **FATHER DONALD** *is saying.)*

Now I'm a religious man, a man of the spirit; but knowledge is knowledge and I must accept what is proven fact whether that fact comes from science or philosophy or whatever. What kind of man are you that you think you can deny it? You're in despair, David, Whether you think of it that way or not. It's only into a valley of ruin that you are trying to lock yourself. You can only die there, David. Accept me. Let God open your eyes; let Him. He will redeem you. Not I nor anyone, but only Him – yet if you reject me, you reject Him, My hand is His. His blessing.

(His hand is rising.)

My blessing. Let me give you my blessing.

(And **DAVID***'s cane strikes* **FATHER DONALD***'s arm.)*

(Crying out.)

FATHER DONALD. *(Cont.)* Owwwww. Let…me…bless you!

(As the hand is rising.)

Please…

> *(**DAVID**, striking again, stands. He hits again and again.)*

David! David! Stop it. Let me bless you.

> *(**DAVID** hits the arm; he hits **FATHER DONALD**'s leg.)*

DAVID. I don't want you here!

FATHER DONALD. You don't know what you're saying.

> *(Now the blow seems about to come straight down on his head. He yells and picks up a chair, holds it up for protection.)*

Stop it. Stop it, goddammit – stop hitting me. Stop it. You are in despair.

> *(Slamming the chair down.)*

A man who hits a priest is in despair!

> *(The cane smacks into his arm.)*

Ohhhhh, this pain – this terrible pain in my arm – I offer it to earn you your salvation.

DAVID. Get out!

FATHER DONALD. Death! Do you understand that. Death! Death is your choice. You are in despair.

> *(Turning to leave.)*

DAVID. And may God reward you, Father.

> *(Stopped by this, **FATHER DONALD** tuns back to find **DAVID**, lighting a cigarette, flopping down on the bed.)*

FATHER DONALD. Oh, yes; yes, of course, you're so confident now, young and strong. Look at you; full of spunk, smiling. But all that will change. Your tune will change in time.

What about pain, Dave? Physical pain. What do you do when it comes? Now you send me away, but in a little while you'll call me back, run down by time, lying with death on your bed in an empty house, gagging on your own spit you cannot swallow; you'll call me then, nothing left to you but fear and Christ's black judging eyes about to find and damn you, you'll call.

DAVID. *(Inhaling and blowing smoke.)* That's not impossible, Father.

FATHER DONALD. I don't even like you; do you know that? I don't even like you.

DAVID. Tell them I hit you when you go down.

FATHER DONALD. *(Near the door, thinking about trying to bless from there.)* No. No, they've pain enough already.

> *(As if he has read* FATHER DONALD*'s mind and knows what the man is thinking,* DAVID*'s cane is rising ready to strike.)*

DAVID. Have they? You get the fuck out of here before I kill you.

FATHER DONALD. *(Not moving a muscle as they face off.)* Though I do not move my hand, I bless you! You are blessed!

> *(*HARRIET *enters from the kitchen, carrying a bucket of cleaning equipment and a feather duster. Then* FATHER DONALD *flees the room, and as he starts down, he sees* HARRIET*, her back to him, dusting the living room.* FATHER DONALD *doesn't want to talk to her at the moment and turns off in the hallway headed for the bathroom.)*

> *(*HARRIET *continues dusting as* RICK *comes in the front door, headed straight for the kitchen.)*

RICK. Hi Mom!

HARRIET. Hi Rick!

So, Ricky, the thing I want to do – I just think it would be so nice if we could get Dave a date with some nice girl.

RICK. *(Having paused to listen.)* Oh, sure.

HARRIET. Do you think that would be a good idea?

> (**OZZIE**, *descending from the attic, peeks into* **DAVID***'s room; he finds* **DAVID** *asleep.)*

RICK. Sure.

HARRIET. Do you know any girls you think might get along with David?

RICK. No, but I still think it's really a good idea and I'll keep it in mind for all the girls I meet and maybe I'll meet one.

> *(Looking up to see* **OZZIE** *on his way down.)*

Here comes Dad. Hi, Dad. Bye, Mom.

HARRIET. Oh, Ozzie, did you see what they were doing?

OZZIE. Dave's sleeping, Harriet; Father Donald's gone.

HARRIET. What? He can't be gone.

OZZIE. I thought maybe he was down here. How about the kitchen?

HARRIET. No, no, I just came out of the kitchen. Where were you, upstairs? Are you sure he wasn't in David's room?

OZZIE. I was in the attic.

HARRIET. Well, maybe he saw the light and came up to join you and you missed each other on the way up and down. Why don't you go check?

OZZIE. I turned off all the lights, Harriet. The attic's dark now.

HARRIET. Well, yell up anyway.

OZZIE. But that attic's dark now, Harriet.

HARRIET. Just in case.

OZZIE. What are you trying to say? – Father Donald's up in the attic in the dark? I mean, if he was up there and I turned off the lights, he'd have said something – "Hey, I'm here," or something. It's stupid to think he wouldn't.

(As he sits down at the table.)

HARRIET. No more stupid to think that than to think he'd leave without telling us what happened with David.

OZZIE. All right, all right

(Storming to the base of the stairs.)

HEEEEEEYYYYYY! UP THERE! ANYBODY UP THERE?

(As there is a brief silence, he turns toward **HARRIET.***)*

DAVID. WHAT'S THAT, DAD?

(On his bed in his room with **ZUNG** *beside him.)*

OZZIE. *(Falters.)* What?

DAVID. WHAT'S UP, DAD?

OZZIE. OH, DAVE, NO, NOT YOU.

DAVID. WHY ARE YOU YELLING?

OZZIE. NO, NO, WE JUST THOUGHT FATHER DONALD WAS UP THERE IN THE ATTIC, DAVE. DON'T YOU WORRY ABOUT IT.

DAVID. I'M THE ONLY ONE UP HERE, DAD!

OZZIE. BUT… YOU'RE NOT IN THE ATTIC, SEE?

DAVID. I'M IN MY ROOM.

OZZIE. I KNOW YOU'RE IN YOUR ROOM.

DAVID. YOU WANT ME TO GO UP IN THE ATTIC?

OZZIE. NO! GODDAMMIT, JUST –

DAVID. I DON'T KNOW WHAT YOU WANT.

OZZIE. I WANT YOU TO SHUT UP, DAVE, THAT'S WHAT I WANT, JUST –

FATHER DONALD. *(Appearing in the hall near the landing.)* What's the matter? What's all the yelling?

HARRIET. Oh, Father!

OZZIE. Father, hello, hello.

HARRIET. How did it go? Did it go all right?

FATHER DONALD. Fine, just fine.

(Coming down the steps, trying to appear as if nothing out of the ordinary has happened.)

HARRIET. Oh, you're perspiring so, though – look at you.

FATHER DONALD. Well, I've got a lot on my mind. It happens. Nerves. I've other appointments. Many, many.

(All this as he is trying to get to the door.)

HARRIET. You mean you're leaving? What are you saying?

FATHER DONALD. I must.

HARRIET. But we've got to talk.

FATHER DONALD. Call me.

HARRIET. Father…bless me…!

FATHER DONALD. *(Alarmed.)* What…?

HARRIET. Bless me…

FATHER DONALD. Of course.

> *(HARRIET bows her head, FATHER DONALD warily blesses her.)*

HARRIET. Ohhh, Father, thank you so much.

> *(Touching his hand.)*

Shall I walk you to your car?

FATHER DONALD. Fine, fine. That's all right. Sure.

> *(Backing for the door.)*

OZZIE. *(Calling up.)* DAVE, SAY "GOODBYE" TO FATHER DONALD, HE'S LEAVING NOW.

FATHER DONALD. GOODBYE, DAVE!

DAVID. GOODBYE, FATHER!

> *(HARRIET and FATHER DONALD go out.)*

> *(OZZIE, after a thoughtful hesitation, rises and climbs the stairs to DAVID's room, where, after hesitating an instant, he gently knocks. DAVID lies with ZUNG, who rises as if to leave, but DAVID keeps her with him.)*

OZZIE. Dave, I'd like to come in…if I could.

(Easing in.)

I mean, first of all, I want to apologize. I don't know why but I feel I ought to. I'm gonna sit down here.

(Indicating the bed, he hesitates, stands.)

Are you awake enough to understand? I am your father, you know, and I could command...if I wanted. I don't; but I could. I'm going to sit...

*(**OZZIE** sits beside **DAVID**, who is now seated on the side of the bed, both facing out, a slight distance between them and **ZUNG** at **DAVID**'s side.)*

I mean, it's so sad the way you just go on and on...and I'd like to have time for you, but you want so much; I have important things, too. I have plans. I'm older, you know; if I fail to fulfill them, who will do it? Not you, though you could. And Rick's too busy. Do you understand? There's no evidence in the world of me – no sign or trace, as if everything I've ever done were no more than smoke. My life has closed behind me like water. But I must not care about it. I must not. Though I have inside me a kind of grandeur I can't realize, many things and memories of a darker time when we were very different – harder – nearer to the air and we thought of nothing as a gift. But I can't make you see that. There's no way. It's what I am, but it's not what you are. Even if I had the guitar, I would only stand here telling my fingers what to do, but they would do nothing. You would not see. I can't get beyond these hands. I jam in the fingers. I break on the bone. I am lonely. I mean, oh, no, not exactly lonely, not really. That's a little strong, actually.

(Silence.)

I mean, Dave...

*(Pulling **DAVID**'s Garrison cap from his back pocket.)*

What's this?

DAVID. What?

OZZIE. This cap. What is it? I almost cut myself on it. I was rummaging in your stuff upstairs, your bag and stuff and I grabbed it. It almost cut me.

(As DAVID is reaching for the cap.)

DAVID. Oh, yes.

OZZIE. There are razors sewn into it. Why is that?

DAVID. To cut people.

(Slowly putting the cap on his head.)

OZZIE. Oh.

DAVID. Here. I'll show you. You're on the street, see. You walk…and see someone who's after you – you wait…

(He tenses, hand rising to the cap.) …as they get near… slowly you remove the hat – they think you're going to toss it aside, see? You… Snap it! You snap it!

(Seizing the front tip of the cap between thumb and finger, he snaps it down. It whistles past OZZIE, who startles.)

It cuts them. They hold their face. However you want them, they're yours. You can stomp them, kick them. This is on the street. I'd like to do that to somebody, wouldn't you?

OZZIE. Huh?

DAVID. It'd be fun.

OZZIE. Oh, sure. I…

DAVID. Who told you to buy this house?

OZZIE. It's a good house. Solid. Not one of those prefabs, those –

DAVID. It's a coffin. You made it big so you wouldn't know, but that's what it is, a coffin, and not all the curtains and pictures and lamps in the world can change it. They threw you off that fast free train, Ozzie.

OZZIE. Best thing that ever happened to me.

DAVID. Do you know, Dad, it seemed sometimes I would rise, and slam with my fists into the walls of a city.

Pointing at buildings, I turned them into fire. I took the fleeing people into my fingers and bent them to touch their heads to their heels, each screaming at the sight of their brain turning black. And now sometimes I miss them, all those screaming people. I wish they were here with us, you and Mom and Rick and Zung and me.

OZZIE. Mom and Rick and who and you, Dave?

DAVID. Zung.

OZZIE. Zung, Dave?

DAVID. She's here. They were all just hunks of meat that had no mind to know of me until I cared for her. It was simple. We lived in a house. She didn't want to come back here, Dad, she wanted me to stay there. And in all the time I knew her, she cost me six dollars that I had to sneak into her purse. Surprise? In time I'll show you some things. You'll see them. I will be your father.

(Tossing the cap at OZZIE.*)*

OZZIE. Pardon, Dave?

(Wincing, cutting himself as he catches the cap.)

DAVID. What's wrong? You sound like something's terribly wrong?

OZZIE. No. No, no. I'm fine.

*(*HARRIET *enters the front door and moves dejectedly across to the kitchen where she enters.)*

Your poor mother – she's why I'm here. Your poor mother, sick with grief. She's mine to care for, you know. It's me you're after, yet you torment her. No more. No more. That's what I came up here to tell you.

DAVID. Good.

OZZIE. What do you mean, "good"? I just told you to stop what you're doing.

*(*HARRIET *comes out of the kitchen with the vacuum cleaner, which she carries and plugs in near the front door.)*

(The light is dimming now into late afternoon.)

DAVID. I know.

OZZIE. You're phony, David – phony – trying to make up for the thousands you butchered, when if you were capable of love at all you would love us, your mother and me – not that we matter –

DAVID. I know.

OZZIE. I want her happy.

DAVID. Of course.

> *(**OZZIE** walks out of the room, and as **HARRIET** turns on the vacuum cleaner and starts to vacuum, he hurries down. He approaches as she works, and then he touches her arm. She looks up expectantly and turns off the vacuum cleaner.)*

HARRIET. Were you talking?

OZZIE. Yes.

HARRIET. Did you have a nice talk?

OZZIE. Harriet, what would you say if I said I wanted some checking done?

HARRIET. I don't know what you mean. In what way do you mean?

OZZIE. Take a look at that. But just be careful.

HARRIET. What is it?

OZZIE. His cap. There are razor blades sewn in it; all along the edge.

HARRIET. Ozzie...ohhh! Goodness.

OZZIE. That's what I mean. And I was reading just yesterday – some of them bring back guns and knives. Bombs. We've got somebody living in this house who's killed people, Harriet, and that's a fact we've got to face. I mean, I think we ought to do some checking. You know that test where they check teeth against old X-rays.

HARRIET. Ohhh, my God...!

OZZIE. I know, I know, it scares me, too, but what are we talking about? We're talking about bombs and guns and knives – and sometimes I don't even think it's David up there. I feel funny sometimes, I mean, and I want his fingerprints taken. I think we should have his blood type –

HARRIET. Oh, Ozzie, it was you.

OZZIE. Huh?

HARRIET. You did it. It was you. You got this out of his luggage, upstairs. You broke in and searched and called the police.

OZZIE. What?

HARRIET. You told them to come here and then you lied and said you didn't.

OZZIE. What? No. No, no.

HARRIET. You did and you lied and now you're lying again. What's wrong with you?

OZZIE. Oh, no. No.

HARRIET. What's happening to you? It's sick and disgusting – to call the police on your own son is sick and disgusting!

OZZIE. But I didn't do it. I didn't. I didn't. No, no. And even if I did what would it mean but I changed my mind, that's all. Sure. I called and then changed my mind and said I didn't when I did, and since when is there anything wrong in that? It would mean only that I have a little problem of ambivalence. I got a minor problem of ambiguity goin' for me here, is all, and you're exaggerating everything all out of proportion. You're distorting everything!

(Headed toward the front door.)

All of you! If I have to lie to live, I will! I'll lie.

(Getting his jacket to leave.)

HARRIET. Where are you going? Come back here, Ozzie. Where are you going? Ozzie?

OZZIE. *(Halfway out the door he stares at her defiantly, a little crazily, lying to her face.)* Kitchen! Kitchen!

(He goes out the front door. **HARRIET**, *alone and stricken, starts to vacuum, again, only to have a sudden tantrum. She is in the midst of her tantrum when* **RICK**, *carrying a bottle of pop, enters from the kitchen.)*

RICK. *(Yelling over the vacuum cleaner.)* Hi, Mom. We're all out of cookies, Mom, and this is the second to last pop.

(**HARRIET** *stares at him and turns off the vacuum.)*

HARRIET. One day, Ricky…there were these two kittens and a puppy all in our backyard fighting. The kittens were little furballs, so angry, and the little puppy, yapping and yapping. I was just a girl, but I picked them up in my arms, I held them all in my arms and they got very, very quiet.

RICK. *(Making sure she hears every word.)* I'm going up to my bedroom to study my history and English and trigonometry, Mom.

HARRIET. Do you know, Father Donald just got into his car and drove away without telling me what happened. He's starting to act like Jesus. You never hear from him. Isn't that funny?

RICK. I'm going up to my bedroom to study my history and English and trigonometry, Mom, okay?

(As **RICK** *bounds away up the stairs.)*

HARRIET. Fine, Ricky. Look in on David, would you?

RICK. Sure.

HARRIET. Good night.

RICK. *(Calling as he passes* **DAVID**'s *door.)* Hi, Dave.

DAVID. Hi, Rick.

RICK. DAVE'S OKAY, MOM.

HARRIET. Thanks, Rick.

(**HARRIET** *unplugs the vacuum cleaner and lugs it across the room, to plug it in near the kitchen door. At the same time,* **DAVID** *and* **ZUNG** *make their*

*way out of his room and climb the stairs toward
the attic. As they go,* **HARRIET** *starts to vacuum
the opposite side of the room. After a beat, the door
bursts open and* **OZZIE** *charges in, very excited,
yelling over the noise of the vacuum cleaner.)*

OZZIE. Harriet! Can you guess what happened? You'll
never guess what happened.

> *(She continues cleaning, and both are yelling over
> the noise of the vacuum cleaner.)*

Harriet, wait; stop.

HARRIET. Ozzie, I've got work to do.

OZZIE. But I want to tell you something.

HARRIET. All right, tell me; I can clean and listen; I can do
both.

> *(He jumps near and steps on the vacuum cleaner
> control, turning it off.)*

OZZIE. Lookit. Look at that. What do you think that is?
That spot on my coat, do you see it? That yellow?

HARRIET. *(Touching the spot.)* Ohhhh, Ozzie…!

OZZIE. And the red mark on my neck.

HARRIET. Ohh, Ozzie, what happened? A bee sting! You
got stung by a bee!

> *(She hurries into the kitchen to get something to
> treat his bee sting.)*

OZZIE. No, no; I was walking – thinking – trying to solve
our problems. Somebody hit me with an egg. They
threw it at me.

> *(As she runs out of the kitchen.)*

I got hit with an egg.

> *(She stares at him.)*

That's right. I was just walking down the street and
– bang – I was hit. I almost blacked out; I almost fell
down.

HARRIET. Ozzie, my God, who would do such a thing?

OZZIE. I don't know. That's the whole point. I've racked
   my brain to understand and I can't. I was just walking
   along. That's all I was doing.

HARRIET. You mean you didn't even see them?

OZZIE. *(Pacing, his excitement growing.)* They were – in a car.
   I saw the car. And I saw the hand, too. Somebody's
   hand. A very large hand. Incredibly large.

HARRIET. What kind of car?

OZZIE. I don't know. An old one – black – big high fenders.

HARRIET. A Buick.

OZZIE. I think so; yes. Cruising up and down, up and down.

HARRIET. Was it near here? Why don't you sit down?

   (Trying to help him sit, to calm and comfort him.)

Sit down. Relax.

   *(He obeys, hardly aware of what he is doing, sort of
   squatting on the couch.)*

OZZIE. And I heard them, too. They were hollering.

HARRIET. What did they say?

OZZIE. I don't know. It was just all noise. I couldn't
   understand.

   (Bounding from the couch to the armchair.)

HARRIET. It was more than one? My God!

OZZIE. *(Too restless to sit anywhere, he's back on his feet.)* I don't
   know. Two at least, at the very least. One to drive and
   one to throw. Maybe even three. A lookout, sort of,
   peering up and down and then he sees me. "There," he
   says; he points me out, I'm strolling along like a stupid
   ass, I don't even see them. The driver picks up speed.
   The thrower cocks his arm…

   (Reliving the story, cocking his arm.)

HARRIET. Ozzie, please, can't you relax? You look awful.

OZZIE. Nooo, I can't relax, goddammit!

HARRIET. You look all flushed and sweating; please.

OZZIE. It just makes me so goddamn mad the more I think about it. It really does. Goddammit! Goddammit!

HARRIET. Oh, you poor thing.

OZZIE. Because it was calculated; it was calculated, Harriet, because that egg had been boiled to just the right point so it was hard enough to hurt but not so hard it wouldn't splatter. The filthy sonsabitches, but I'm gonna find 'em, I swear that to God, I'm gonna find 'em. I'm gonna kill 'em. I'm gonna cut out their hearts!

> *(RICK appears at the top of the stairs, playing his guitar.)*

RICK. – Hey! What's all the racket? What's –

OZZIE. Ricky, come down here! – Goddamn 'em!

HARRIET. Ricky, somebody hit your father with an egg!

RICK. Hit him?

> *(Descending hurriedly.)*

Hit Dad?

OZZIE. They just threw it! Where's Dave? Dave here?

> *(Suddenly looking around, moving for the stairs.)*

I wanna tell Dave. DAVE!

HARRIET. Ozzie, give me your jacket!

> *(Following him, tugging at the jacket.)*

OZZIE. I wanna tell Dave!

> *(Struggling to help get the jacket off.)*

HARRIET. I'll take the spot off.

OZZIE. I gotta tell ole Dave!

> *(Climbing rapidly, checking in on DAVID's empty room.)*

Dave? Dave?

> *(Hurrying on up in the direction of the attic.)*

OZZIE. Hey, Dave? Dave! David!

(As **HARRIET** *sits down on the couch with a can of spot remover removed from the bucket of cleaning items she brought in earlier, and* **RICK** *joins her.)*

RICK. Boy, that's something, huh. What you got there, Mom?

HARRIET. *(As she works on the jacket.)* Meyer Spot Remover, it's the best. It gives just a sprinkling…like snow, which brushed away, leaves the fabric clean and fresh like spring.

(**OZZIE** *and* **DAVID** *are rushing down the stairs, as* **ZUNG** *trails them.)*

OZZIE. I got hit by an egg. And then there's this car tearin' off up the street, Christ. Jesus, I said, I just been hit with an egg. Jesus Christ, that's impossible, and the way I felt – the way I feel – Harriet, let's have some beer; let's have some good beer for the boys and me.

(With a sigh, **HARRIET** *moves to obey; she will bring beer; she will bring peanuts.* **OZZIE** *is pleased with his high energy, with his being the center of attention as he has, it seems, the attention of his two sons seated on the couch.)*

(It's early evening now, the room darkened a bit, and **OZZIE** *turns on the living room light switch.)*

It took me back to when I was a kid. Ole Fat Kramer. He lived on my street and we used to fight every day. For fun. Monday he'd win, and Tuesday, I'd beat him silly, my knees on his shoulders, blam, blam, blam. Later on, he grew up, became a merchant marine, sailed all over the world, and then he used to race sailboats up and down both coasts – he had one he lived on – anything that floated, he wanted to sail it. And he wasn't fat either. We just called him that; and boy, oh boy, if he was around now – ohhhh, would we go get those punks threw that egg at me. We'd run 'em into the ground. We'd kill 'em like dogs, poor little stupid ugly dogs, we'd cut out their hearts.

RICK. *(Suddenly getting to his feet and gliding toward the door.)* Excuse me, Dad; excuse me. Listen, I've got to get going. You don't mind, do you. Got places to go; you're just talking about the past anyway. Bye Mom! Bye Dad!

> *(On his way to the door.)*

HARRIET. Have a good time, Rick.

RICK. I'm too pretty not to, Mom!

> *(He goes out the door, and* OZZIE *follows him up to the door.)*

OZZIE. Where is he going? Where does he always go? Why does he always go and have some place to go? Always!

HARRIET. Just you never mind, Ozzie. He's young and you're not. I'm going to do the dishes, but you just go right ahead with your little story and I'll listen from the kitchen.

> *(Gathering the empty beer bottles and glasses, she goes into the kitchen.)*

OZZIE. I…out-ran a bowling ball once. They bet I couldn't, but I – but – I –

> *(Settling down at the kitchen table,* OZZIE *finds* DAVID *appearing to stare at him. They face each other silently, as* ZUNG *descends to sit beside him.)*

What are you looking at? What do you think you're seeing?

DAVID. I'm not looking.

OZZIE. I feel watched; looked at.

DAVID. No.

OZZIE. Observed.

DAVID. I'm blind.

OZZIE. Did you do it? Had you anything to do with it?

DAVID. What?

OZZIE. That egg.

DAVID. I can't see.

OZZIE. I think you did. I feel like you did it.

DAVID. I don't have a car. I can't drive. How could I?

HARRIET. *(Popping in from the kitchen to unplug the vacuum cleaner.)* Ohh, it's so good to hear men's voices in the house again, two of my three favorite men in all the world, it's what I live for, really. Would you like some coffee? Oh, of course you would. Let me put some on. Your humble servant at your command, I do your bidding, bid me be gone.

> *(Taking the vacuum cleaner back into the kitchen, she is gone.)*

OZZIE. *(Still fixed on **DAVID**.)* I could run again if I wanted. I'd like…to want to. Christ, Fat Kramer is probably dead now – not bouncing about in the ocean in some rattletrap, tin-can joke of a ship…but dust…locked in a box…held in old…cold hands. And I just stand here, don't I, and let you talk any way you want. And Ricky gets up in the middle of some sentence I'm saying and walks right out and I let him. Because I'm afraid of him, just as I fear your mom…and you. Because I know the time is close when I will be of no use to any of you any longer; and so I'm frightened that if I do not seem inoffensive…and pleasant…if I am not careful to never disturb any of you unnecessarily, you will all abandon me. I can no longer compel recognition. I can no longer impose myself; make myself seen.

HARRIET. *(Entering, happily, with a tray of coffee.)* Here you go. One for each and tea for me. Cream for David…

> *(Setting a cup for **DAVID**, moving to serve **OZZIE**.)*

…and cream and sugar for –

OZZIE. Christ, how you must have beguiled me!

HARRIET. Pardon?

OZZIE. Beguiled and deceived!

HARRIET. Pardon… Ozzie…?

OZZIE. And I don't even remember. I say "must" because I don't remember, I was so innocent, so childish in my strength, never seeing that it was surrendering I was doing, innocently and easily giving to you the love that was to return in time as flesh to imprison, detain, disarm and begin…to kill.

HARRIET. Ozzie, how many beers have you had? You've had too many beers!

OZZIE. Get away!

> *(Whirling to point at* **DAVID** *on the couch,* **ZUNG** *beside him.)*

Shut up! You've said enough! Detain and kill! Take and give nothing. It's what you meant, isn't it. You said it, a warning, nearly exactly this. This is your meaning!

DAVID. You're doing so well, Dad.

OZZIE. What?

DAVID. You're doing so well.

OZZIE. No.

DAVID. You are.

OZZIE. I'm doing awful. I'm doing terrible.

DAVID. This is the way you start, Dad. We'll be runners. Dad and Dave!

OZZIE. What's he saying?

HARRIET. *(Moving to* **OZZIE,** *trying to console him.)* My God, you're shaking; you're shaking.

OZZIE. I don't know what he's talking about. What's he talking about?

> *(Warning* **HARRIET** *away as she tries to soothe him.)*

Just let me alone. Just please let me be. I don't really mean these things I'm saying. They're not really important. They'll go away and I don't mean them; they're just coming out of me, I'm just saying them, but I don't mean them. Oh, please, please, go away.

> *(Retreating from her.)*

> *(***DAVID** *rises, and with* **ZUNG,** *starts up the stairs.* **HARRIET** *is startled by his movement.)*

HARRIET. David?

DAVID. I'm going upstairs.

HARRIET. Oh, yes. Of course, of course.

DAVID. Just for a while.

HARRIET. Fine. Good. Of course.

DAVID. I'll see you all later.

(*He and* **ZUNG** *climb to the attic.*)

OZZIE. I remember. There was a day…when I wanted to leave you, all of you, and I wanted desperately to leave, and I thought, "No. No," I couldn't. "Think of the children," I said. I meant something by that. I meant something and I understood it. But now… I don't. I no longer have it – that understanding. It's left me. What did I mean?

(*Ending up on the couch.*)

HARRIET. (*Approaching.*) You're trembling again. Look at you.

OZZIE. For a while – just a while, stay away. That's all I ask.

HARRIET. (*Sitting beside him, reaching to touch him.*) What?

OZZIE. Stay the hell away from me!

HARRIET. Stay away? How far away, Ozzie? How far away? I'll move over…

(*Both hurt and defiant, she slides away on the couch.*)

…here. Is this far enough away? Ozzie?

OZZIE. It's my hands; my feet. There's tiredness in me. I wake up each morning, it's in my fingers…sleep…

HARRIET. Ohhh, it's such a hateful thing in you the way you have no love for people different than yourself, even when your son has come home to tell you of them; you have no right to carry on this way. He didn't bring her back – didn't marry her – we have those two things to thank God for. You've got to stop thinking only of yourself. We don't matter, only the children. When are you going to straighten out your thinking? You've got to straighten out your thinking.

OZZIE. I do. I know.

HARRIET. We don't matter; we're nothing. You're nothing, Ozzie. Only the children.

OZZIE. I know. I promise.

HARRIET. All right. Just…rest. For a little; I'll be back.

OZZIE. I promise, Harriet.

HARRIET. I'll go see how he is.

(Rising.)

OZZIE. *(Coiled on the couch.)* It's my hands; they hurt. I want to wrap them; my feet.

HARRIET. *(Moving partway up the stairs.)* I'll tell him for you. I'll explain – how you didn't mean those terrible things you said. I'll explain.

OZZIE. It's going to be so cold; and I hurt…already; so cold; my ankles!

(**HARRIET** *hurries back to* **OZZIE** *and begins to cover and tuck him in with an afghan that has been draped over the back of the couch.)*

HARRIET. *(Taking care of him, tucking him in.)* Oh, Ozzie, Ozzie, we're all so worried, but I just think we must hope for the fine bright day coming when we'll be a family again as long as we try for what is good, truly for one another. Please.

(She hurries up to the landing, where she then goes down the hall toward the bathroom. After a beat, **RICK** *comes in.)*

RICK. *(Cheery.)* Hi, Mom; hi, Dad.

OZZIE. *(Lying on the couch, wrapped in the afghan.)* Hi, Rick. Your mom's upstairs. You have a nice time? I bet you did.

RICK. Fine; sure. How about you?

OZZIE. Fine; sure.

RICK. Whata you doin' – restin'?

OZZIE. *(Still on the couch, wrapped in the afghan.)* Workin'. Measurin'. Not everybody can play the guitar, you know. I'm going to build a wall, I think. A wall. Pretty soon. Or…six walls. Thinkin' through the blueprints; lookin' over the plans.

RICK. *(Moving for the kitchen.)* I'm gonna get some fudge, you want some?

OZZIE. No. Too busy.

> *(**RICK** pops in and out of the kitchen almost instantly. Chewing a piece of fudge he sits down on the couch near **OZZIE**, strumming his guitar for a few seconds.)*

RICK. I just had the greatest piece o' tail, Dad.

OZZIE. What?

RICK. I really did. What a beautiful piece o' ass.

OZZIE. Just now?

RICK. She was bee-auuuuu-ti-ful.

OZZIE. Who was it?

RICK. Nobody you'd know, Dad.

OZZIE. Oh. Where'd you do it – I mean, get it.

RICK. In her car.

OZZIE. You were careful, I hope.

RICK. C'mon, Dad.

> *(Laughing a little.)*

OZZIE. I mean, it wasn't any decent girl.

RICK. Hell, no…

> *(**RICK** is still chuckling, as **OZZIE** gets to his feet.)*

OZZIE. Had a dream of the guitar last night. It was huge as a building – all flecked with ice. You swung it in the air and I exploded.

RICK. I did?

OZZIE. Yes. I was gone.

RICK. Fantastic.

> *(As **OZZIE** approaches the front door.)*

Where you goin', Dad? You going out?

OZZIE. Looks like it.

> (**OZZIE** *goes out the front door.*)

RICK. Night, Dad.

> (*It's night now, the world darkening outside as* **RICK** *sits alone in lowering light on the couch, strumming, and the tune changes to something soft and lyrical.*)

> (**HARRIET** *comes down the hall toward* **DAVID**'s *dark room. She carries a towel, soap, a basin of water. She raps on the door with their special knocking that invites a response from* **DAVID**, *which he answers with two knocks. Cheered by this, feeling invited in, she enters, smiling.* **ZUNG** *sits on the chair in the shadowy corner.* **HARRIET** *throws a wall switch to turn the room light on and finds* **DAVID** *in bed, smoking a cigarette.*)

HARRIET. A little bath… David? A little sponge bath, all right? You must be all hot and sticky, always in that bed. And we can talk. Why don't you take your shirt off?

> (*As she sets the basin down and tries to remove his blanket, he holds it back and a little game of tug of war ensues.*)

We've an awful lot to talk about. Take your shirt off, David. Your poor father – he has no patience; no strength. Something has to be done… A little sponge bath would be so nice. Have you talked to him lately? I think he thinks you're angry, for instance, with… us…for some reason. I don't know. Take your shirt off, David. You'll feel cool.

> (*Seated beside him, she bathes him, tenderly, little kisses as if he were a baby.*)

HARRIET. That's all we've ever wanted, your father and me – good sweet things for you and Rick – ease and lovely children, a car, a wife, a good job. Time to relax

and go to church on Sundays…and on holidays all the
children and grandchildren come together, mingling –
it would be so wonderful – everyone so happy – turkey.
Twinkling lights.

*(Playfully, getting behind him and raising his
arms.)*

David, are you going to take your shirt off for me?

(She tugs his shirt off.)

DAVID. They hit their children, did you know that? They
hit them with sticks.

HARRIET. What?

*(As she places the basin of water on his lap and
kneels before him to wash his belly, his chest.)*

DAVID. The yellow people. They punish the disobedience
of their children with sticks. And then they sleep
together one family in a bed, limbs all entwined like
puppies. They work.

I've seen them…laugh. They go on picnics. They
murder – out of petty jealousy. Young girls wet their
cunts with spit when they are dry from wear and yet
another GI stands in line. They spit on their hands and
rub themselves, smiling, opening their arms.

HARRIET. That's not true.

*(Playfully, she dabs at his mouth, as if to wash it
of what he's said.)*

DAVID. Why do you say that?

HARRIET. Because it isn't.

(Dabbing playfully on his mouth and face.)

None of what you say. No. No. All you did was
something normal and regular, can't you see? And
hundreds of boys have done it before you. Thousands
and thousands. Even now. Now. Now. Why do you have
to be so sick and morbid about something so ordinary?

*(Below in the dark, **RICK** continues to strum the lyrical melody; sweet, melancholy, and repetitive.)*

*(Moving to sit on the bed beside **DAVID**.)*

Oh, David, David, I'm sure she was a lovely little girl, but I would be insane if I didn't want you to marry someone of your own with whom you could be happy – if I didn't want grandchildren who could be free and welcome in their world. I couldn't want anything else and still think I loved you. David, think of their faces, their poor funny little faces…

DAVID. I know… I know…

*(**DAVID** is moving his cane slowly along the floor, so the tip grazes her ankle and then climbs slowly.)*

HARRIET. The human face was not meant to be that way.

(She dabs his nose, his eyes, as she speaks, all tenderly, his mouth.)

A nose is a thinness – you know that, and the lips that are not thin are ugly, and it is we who disappear, David. They don't change and we are gone. It is our triumph, our whiteness. We disappear.

(The cane rises under the hem of her dress, lifting, and she can no longer ignore it.)

What are you doing? They take us back and down if our children are theirs – it is not a mingling of blood, it is theft.

(She recoils and pushes the cane away and stands, and he follows, backing her toward the door.)

Oh, you don't mean these awful things you do – your room stinks – odors come from under the door. You don't clean yourself. David, David, you've lost someone you love and it's pain for you, don't you see? I know, I know. But we will be the same, lost from you – you from us – and what will that gain for anyone? What?

DAVID. Do you remember – ?

HARRIET. No. No!

(**DAVID** *grabs her and throws her onto the bed.*)

DAVID. I know you do.

HARRIET. I don't.

DAVID. (*Following, pinning her down.*) Of course you do. It was a Sunday morning and we had all gone to church like we always did on Sunday mornings, going to mass; and there was a young man there with his yellow wife and child. You spoke to us, when we left the church… to Dad and Rick and me, as if we were conspirators. "I feel so sorry for that poor man – the baby looks like her," you said and your mouth twisted as if you had been forced to swallow someone else's spit.

HARRIET. I want to go outside. I want to go outside and walk.

DAVID. Do you remember? How much do you remember?

HARRIET. You want only to hurt us, don't you. Isn't that right? That's all you want. Only to give us unhappiness. You cheat her, David. That lovely, lovely little girl you spoke of. She merits more to be done in her memory than cruelty.

> (**HARRIET** *tries to get away, almost getting away, but* **DAVID** *flings her down on the bed, pinning her there.*)

DAVID. (*Anguished at it all.*) It seemed that I should go to her if I was to ever live, and I felt that if I ever truly touched her secret stranger's tongue and mind, I would somehow die. Now she will not forgive me for the way I was.

> (*He releases her and she flees for the door.*)

HARRIET. No. No, no. No, you don't know how badly I feel. I've got a fever, the start of a cold or flu. Let me be. I can hardly…move. Or stand up.

> (*Backing into the hall, as he follows.*)

I just want to flop somewhere and not have to move. I'm so weak. Don't hurt me anymore. Don't hurt me

– no more – I've got fever; please. Fever. Don't hurt me.

DAVID. But I have so much to tell you, to show you.

HARRIET. Who are you? I don't know who you are.

DAVID. David.

HARRIET. No.

DAVID. But I am.

HARRIET. No, no. Oh, no.

> *(She backs off down the hall, leaving* **DAVID** *on the landing.* **ZUNG** *stands in the room behind him.)*

DAVID. But it's what you want, don't you see?

> *(Reaching back to* **ZUNG**, *who walks to join him.)*

You can do it.

> *(As* **ZUNG** *moves to him, he takes her in his arms and they dance, slowly, the light red upon them,* **RICK**'s *music from below their song.)*

Her wrists are bound in coils of flowers. Flowers strung in her hair, she hangs from the wind and men strike and kick her. They are blind so that they may not see her, yet they howl, wanting not to hurt her but only as I do, to touch and hold her and they howl.

> *(Dancing sweetly with her in his arms.)*

I'm home. Little David. Home.

> *(Longingly, home at last, holding her and dancing.)*

Little Davey...of all the toys and tops and sailor suits, the plastic cards and Tinkertoys. Drum player, bed wetter, home-run hitter, I'm home...now...and I want to drink from the toilet, wash there.

> *(Eyeing* **RICK** *who plays below, looking up at* **DAVID** *and* **ZUNG**.)*

And you will join me. You...will...join me!

(**RICK** *goes into the kitchen, and* **DAVID** *and* **ZUNG** *climb the stairs toward the attic.*)

(*The front door opens and* **OZZIE** *enters. Under his arm, he carries a packet of several hundred sheets of paper. He moves now with an absolute kind of confidence, almost smugness, as he carefully sets down the papers and proceeds to arrange three of the four kitchen chairs, addressing them as* "**HARRIET,**" "**DAVID,**" *and* "**RICKY.**" *He pats them, arranges them to face him in the manner of the chairman of the board addressing his underlings as he explains his position and plan of action for total solution.*)

OZZIE. (*Looking them over, the three empty chairs.*) Harriet. David. Ricky.

I'm glad we've finally gotten together here, because the thing I've decided to do – and you all, hopefully, will understand my reasoning – is to combat the weariness beginning in me. It's like stepping into a hole, the way I feel each morning when I awaken, I see the day and the sun and I'm looking upward into the sky with a sense of looking down. A sense of hovering over a great pit into which I am about to fall. The sky. Foolishness and deceit, you say, and I know you're right; a trick of feeling inside me being played against me seeking to diminish me and increase itself until it is larger than me filling me and who will I be then? It. That feeling of being nothing. At first...at first I thought the thing to do would be to learn the guitar. But that I realized – in just the nick of time – was a folly that would have taken me into the very agony of frustration I was seeking to avoid. The skill to play like Ricky does is a great gift, and only Ricky has it. He has no acids rotting his heart. He is all lies and music, his brain small and scaly, the brain of a snake forever innocent of the fact that it crawls. Lucky Ricky. But there are other things that people can do. And I've come at last to see the one that I must try if I am to become strong again in my opinion of myself.

(Holding up with supreme confidence one of the many packets of paper.)

OZZIE What I have here is an inventory of everything I own. Everything. Every stick of furniture, pot and pan, every sock, T-shirt, pen, or pencil. And opposite it is its price. For instance – here – that couch – $174.95. That chair – $99.95. That table – $32.29. Et cetera. Et cetera. And here's my portfolio summarized. My mortgage. Life insurance! Now the idea is that you each carry a number of these at all times.

(He is now distributing more papers to the chairs, his control diminishing, so that he is somewhat chaotic.)

Two or three copies, at all times, and you are to pass them out at the slightest provocation. Let people know who I am, what I've done. Someone says to you, "Who are you?" You say, "I'm Ozzie's Son." "I'm Ozzie's Wife." "Who?" they'll say. "Take a look at that!" You tell 'em. Spit it out, give 'em a copy, turn on your heel and walk right out.

*(As **ZUNG** enters from the kitchen, crosses and sits down in one of the empty chairs at the table beside **OZZIE**. She is dressed in contemporary American clothes that **HARRIET** might wear.)*

That's the way I want it; from all of you from here on out, that's the way I want it!

(Taking a breath, he faces her.)

Let him alone. Let David alone.

*(As **HARRIET** walks the upstairs hallway, moving to the stairs to come down.)*

HARRIET. Is there any aspirin down there? I don't feel well… Ozzie. I don't feel well at all. David poked me with his cane and I don't like what's going on.

*(**OZZIE** continues to stare at **ZUNG**.)*

HARRIET. I don't want what's happening to happen. It must be some awful flu. I'm so weak, or some awful cold. There's an odor...

OZZIE. *(Rising.)* I'll go to the drugstore. My eyes hurt funny...

HARRIET. Oh, Ozzie...oh my God. It was awful. I can't help it. He's crazy – he –

OZZIE. I don't want to hear about him. I don't want to hear. Oh, no, oh, no. I can't. No more, no more. Let him do what he wants. No more of him; no more. Just you – you're all that I can see. All that I care for or want.

> *(As* **HARRIET** *and* **OZZIE** *move to each other behind the couch, and they embrace.)*

HARRIET. David's crazy!

OZZIE. You're everything.

HARRIET. Please...

OZZIE. Listen; we must hide; please.

HARRIET. Pray with me.

> *(Kneeling as* **OZZIE**, *helping her, kneels too.)*

OZZIE. We won't move. We'll hide by not moving.

HARRIET. We must beg God to not turn against him; convince Him. Ozzie, pray!

OZZIE. Yes!

HARRIET. Now.

> *(They pray: kneeling, behind the couch, murmuring, and it goes on. The kitchen door opens and* **RICK** *comes in.)*

RICK. Hi, Mom. Hi, Dad.

> *(As they continue praying, he stops, stares, puzzled.)*

Hi... Mom. Hi, Dad...

> *(Quite loud now, demanding a response.)*

Hi... Mom. Hi... Dad...

(He thinks and then looks up the stairs.)

RICK David! What is going on here? What do you think you're doing?

(He goes running up the stairs into DAVID's room, flinging open the door, but the room is empty. Then DAVID comes down out of the attic, dressed in ragged combat fatigues, a headband, towel on his neck as he hurries down the stairs without stopping.)

Dave... Dave, What have you got to say for yourself? What can you?

(As RICK follows DAVID down the stairs, DAVID flops down in the recliner, his father's chair, and ZUNG moves to sit on his lap.)

Honest ta God, I've had it. I really have. I can't help it, even if you are sick, and I hate to complain, but you're getting them so mixed up they're not themselves anymore. They were on their knees, do you know that?

Right here on the living room floor, now what's the point of that? They're my mom and dad, too.

DAVID. He doesn't know, does he, Dad? Did you hear him?

RICK. Let Dad alone.

DAVID. He doesn't know how when you finally see yourself, there's nothing really there to see. Isn't that right? Mom?

RICK. Dave, honest to God, I'm warning you, let them alone.

(OZZIE and HARRIET still kneel behind the couch. DAVID sits with ZUNG on his lap.)

DAVID. Do you know how north of here on farms gentle loving dogs are raised, while in the forests other dogs run wild. And upon occasion, one of those that's wild is captured and put in among the others that are tame, bringing with it the memory of when they had all been wild – the dark and terror – that had made them wolves. Don't you hear them?

(And there is a rumbling.)

RICK. What? Hear what?

(It is the storm-like rumbling of many trucks outside, getting closer and louder.)

DAVID. Don't you hear the trucks? They're all over town, lined up from the center of town into the country. Don't you hear? They've stopped bringing back the blind. They're bringing back the dead now. The convoy's broken up. There's no control. They're walking from house to house, through the shrubbery, under the trees, carrying one of the dead in a bright blue rubber bag for which they have no papers, no name or number. No one knows whose it is. They're at the Jensens' now. Now Al Jensen's at the door, all his kids behind him trying to peek. Al looks for a long, long time into the open bag before he shakes his head. They zipper shut the bag and turn away. They've been to the Mayers', the Kellys', the Irwins' and Kresses'. They'll be here soon.

OZZIE. No.

DAVID. And Dad's going to let them in. We're going to let them in.

HARRIET. What's he saying?

DAVID. He's going to knock.

OZZIE. I don't know.

DAVID. Yes. Yes.

(Loud knocking at the front door.)

OZZIE. Noooooooo.

RICK. Mom, he's driving Dad crazy.

(More knocking.)

OZZIE. David, will I die?

HARRIET. Who do you suppose it could be so late?

RICK. I don't think you should just go opening the door to anybody this time of the night, there's no telling who it might be.

(As **OZZIE** *rises as if to go to the door,* **RICK** *and* **HARRIET** *stop him and move him to sit on the couch where* **HARRIET** *huddles with him.)*

DAVID. We know who it is.

OZZIE. Oh, David, why can't you wait? Why can't you rest?

DAVID. Look at her. See her, Dad.

(Up now, emphatic, triumphant, sure they are about to see the truth.)

Tell her to go to the door. Tell her yes, it's your house, you want her to open the door and let them in. Tell her yes, the one with no name is ours. We'll put it in that chair. They're all ours. We can bring them all here. I want them all here, all the trucks and bodies. There's room. Ricky can sing.

(Handing **RICK** *the guitar.)*

I won't miss them anymore. We'll stack them along the walls…

OZZIE. Nooo…

DAVID. Pile them over the floor…

OZZIE. …No, no…

DAVID. They will become the floor and they will become the walls, the chairs. We'll sit in them, sleep in them. We will call them "home." We will give them as gifts, call them "ring" and "pot" and "cup." No, no; it's not a thing to fear…we will notice them no more than all the others.

OZZIE. What others? There are no others.

(Scurrying to the TV.)

I'll get it fixed. I'll fix it. Who needs to hear it? We'll just watch it.

(As he touches the TV, the sound comes on suddenly.)

Ahhh, it's working!

*(**OZZIE** wildly turns TV channels.)*

OZZIE. I flick my rotten life.

> *(Turning a channel, checking with* **HARRIET** *who shakes her head.)*

No.

> *(Again turning the channel, checking with* **HARRIET***, who shakes her head.)*

No.

> *(Turning the channel as horror movie music comes on, even a scream.)*

Oh, there's a good one. Look at that one. Ohhh, isn't that a good one? That's the best one. That's the best one.

> *(***OZZIE** *hurries back to the couch to watch, and* **DAVID** *steps in front of the screen and then moves in on* **OZZIE** *and* **HARRIET***.)*

DAVID. They will call it madness. We will call it seeing.

OZZIE. I don't want to disappear.

DAVID. *(Intensely at* **OZZIE***.)* Let her take you to the door. We will be runners. You will have eyes.

OZZIE. I will be blind. I will disappear.

DAVID. No.

OZZIE. Ricky, help me.

DAVID. Don't call to him! We don't need him – we –

OZZIE. Ricky!

RICK. No! Let Dad alone!

> *(Leaping from behind* **DAVID***, smashing his guitar down on* **DAVID***'s head; pieces fly and* **DAVID** *crumples.)*

Let him alone. He's sick of you.

> *(Kicking* **DAVID***, dropping on him, slamming his head down on the floor.)*

He's sick of you and all the stupid stuff you talk about. What the hell's a matter with you? He doesn't wanna

talk anymore about all the stupid stuff you talk about…
He wants to talk about cake and cookies and cars and
coffee. He's sick a you and he wants you to shut up. We
hate you, goddamn you.

*(He slams DAVID's head one last time and DAVID
lies still. ZUNG faces OZZIE who stands beside her.)*

ZUNG. *Chào Ông. Chào Ông!* Hôm nay ông manh không?

OZZIE. Oh, what is it that you want? I'm tired, I mean it.
Forgive me. I'm sick of the sight of you, squatting all
the time. In filth, like animals, talking gibberish, your
breath sick with rot… And yet you look at me with
those sad appealing eyes as if there is some real thing
that can come between us when you're not even here.
You are deceit.

*(His hands close on her throat, and he forces her
to the floor.)*

I'm not David. I'm not silly and soft little David. The
sight of you sickens me. You hear me, David? Believe
me. I am speaking my honest true feelings. I spit on
you, the both of you, I piss on your eyes and pain. Flesh
is lies. You are garbage and filth. You are darkness. I cast
you down. Deceit. Animal. Dirty…animal…animal.

*(He is over her, choking her, until they are sprawled.
ZUNG lies there. Silence. OZZIE and HARRIET
meet eyes, and she rises and starts for the kitchen.)*

RICK. I saw this really funny movie last night. This really…
funny, funny movie about this young couple and they
were going to get a divorce but they didn't. It was really
funny.

HARRIET. *(Off in the kitchen.)* What's that? What's that?

RICK. This movie I saw.

*(HARRIET coming back in with a large green
garbage bag, which she shakes open and delivers
to OZZIE.)*

HARRIET. Anybody want to go for groceries? We need
Kleenex, sugar, milk.

RICK. What a really funny movie.

>(OZZIE *and he begin to put* ZUNG *into the bag.*)

OZZIE. I'll go; I'll go.

HARRIET. Good. Good.

OZZIE. I think I saw it on TV.

HARRIET. Did you enjoy it, Rick?

RICK. Oh, yeah. I loved it.

>(OZZIE *drags* ZUNG *in the garbage bag toward the kitchen door, while* HARRIET *clears the way and holds the door open for him.*)

OZZIE. I laughed so much I almost got sick. It was really good. I laughed. And I kept laughing.

RICK. I bet it was; I bet you did.

OZZIE. Oh, I did. And I even realized I was laughing so hard I might get sick, but I kept on laughing that's how funny it was.

>(OZZIE *is gone into the kitchen with* ZUNG. DAVID *is staggering to his feet, staggering about.* HARRIET *lets the kitchen door close.*)

HARRIET. How are you feeling, Ricky?

RICK. Fine.

HARRIET. Good.

RICK. How do you feel?

HARRIET. Oh, I'm all right. I feel fine.

OZZIE. (*Emerging from the kitchen.*) Me, too. I feel fine, too. What day is it, anyway? Monday?

>(*Settling down in the recliner.*)

HARRIET. Wednesday.

>(*Settling on the arm of* OZZIE*'s chair.*)

RICK. Tuesday, Mom.

OZZIE. I thought it was Monday.

RICK. Oh, no.

HARRIET. *(Looking up at the bewildered* DAVID.*)* No, no. You're home now, David…

> *(As* RICK *indicates the seat beside him on the couch,* DAVID *sits.)*

RICK. Hey, Dave, listen, will you, I mean I know it's not my place to speak out and give advice and everything because I'm the youngest, but I just gotta say my honest true feelings and I'd kill myself if I were you, Dave. You're in too much misery. I'd cut my wrists. Honestly speaking, brother to brother, you should have done it long ago. –

> *(As* DAVID *is looking about.)*

You looking for her? She's not here.

DAVID. What?

RICK. Nooo. She's never been here. You just thought so. You decided, Dave, remember? You decided, all things considered, that you preferred to come back without her. Too much risk and inconvenience…you decided. Isn't that right? Sure. You know it is. You've always known. Do you want to use my razor, Dave? I have one right here and you can use it if you want.

> *(Taking a straight razor from his pocket.)*

Just take it if you want it, Dave.

HARRIET. Go ahead, David. The front yard's empty. You don't have to be afraid. The streets, too, still and empty.

RICK. It doesn't hurt like you think it will. Go ahead; just take it, Dave.

OZZIE. You might as well.

RICK. That's right.

OZZIE. You'll feel better.

RICK. I'll help you now, Dave, okay.

> *(As* RICK *starts to help* DAVID *place the razor on his wrist as if ready to cut,* HARRIET *startles.)*

HARRIET. I'll go get some pans and towels.

(Hurrying to the kitchen.)

RICK. *(Patting* DAVID, *very friendly.)* Oh, you're "so confused, you don't know what to do." It's just a good thing I got this razor, boy, that's all I gotta say. You're so confused. You see, Dave, where you're wrong is your point of view, it's silly. It's just really comical because you think people are valuable or something; and given a chance like you were to mess with 'em, to take a young girl like that and turn her into a whore, you shouldn't when of course you should or at least might...on a whim...you see? I mean, you're all backwards, Dave. You're upside down. You don't know how to go easy and play –

> *(HARRIET has brought two silver pans and towels, and as* RICK *talked she has placed the towels on the coffee table and his lap, the two pans, one for each wrist, on the towels on the coffee table. The pans will catch the blood. After all is neatly placed, she sits on the couch beside* DAVID, *as* DAVID, *with* RICK*'s help, will cut one wrist, then the other.)*

I bet you didn't have any fun the whole time you were over there – no fun at all – and it was there. I got this buddy, Gerry, he was there, and he used to throw bags of cement at 'em from off the back a his truck. They'd go whizzin' through those villages, throwin' off these bags a cement. You could kill people, he says, you hit 'em right. Especially the kids. There was this once they knocked this ole man off his bicycle – fifty pounds a dry cement – and then the back a the truck got his legs. It was hysterical – can't you just see that, Dave? Him layin' there howlin', all the guys in the truck bowin' and wavin' and tippin' their hats. What a goddamn funny story, huh?

DAVID. *(Bleeding now.)* I wanted...to kill you...all of you.

RICK. I know, I know; but you're too hurt; too weak.

DAVID. I wanted for you to need what I had and wouldn't give it.

HARRIET. That's not possible.

OZZIE. Nooooo.

DAVID. I wanted to get you. Like poor bug-eyed fish flung up from the brief water to the lasting dirt, I would gut you.

HARRIET. David, no, no, you didn't want that.

OZZIE. No, no.

RICK. I don't even know why you'd think you did.

OZZIE. We kill you is what happens.

RICK. That's right.

OZZIE. And then, of course, we die, too. Later on, I mean. And nothing stops it. Not words or walls or even guitars.

RICK. Sure.

OZZIE. That's what happens.

HARRIET. It isn't too bad, is it?

RICK. How bad is it?

OZZIE. He's getting weaker.

HARRIET. And in a little, it'll all be over. You'll feel so grand. No more funny talk.

RICK. You can shower; put on clean clothes. I've got deodorant you can borrow. "After Roses," Dave. The scent of a thousand roses.

(Preparing to take a picture; crouching before **DAVID.** *)*

HARRIET. Take off your glasses, David.

OZZIE. Do as you're told.

(As **DAVID** *removes the glasses.)*

RICK. I bet when you were away there was only plain water to wash in huh? You probably had a wash in the rain.

*(***RICK** *takes the picture. Flash; slide appears on the walls of* **DAVID** *'s room. A large close-up of* **DAVID** *'s face appears, his eyes visible for the first time. It is there briefly and then gone.* **RICK** *strums the guitar.)*

RICK. Mom, I like David like this.

HARRIET. He's happier.

    (*As* **DAVID** *sags to the side, his head sinking onto his mother's shoulder as she strokes his brow.*)

OZZIE. We're all happier.

RICK. Too bad he's gonna die.

    (**RICK** *strums more; maybe all this last strumming is the introduction to a '70s song.*)

OZZIE. No, no; he's not gonna die, Rick. He's only gonna nearly die. Only nearly.

RICK. Ohhhhhh.

HARRIET. Mmmmnummm.

    (*And* **RICK** *strums away, and then there's a burst of music as a song from the '70s begins.*)

    (*Blackout as the music continues.*)

End of Play

Sticks and Bones

Music: Galt MacDermot
Lyrics: David Rabe

Baby When I Find You

Ba-by, when I find you, nev-er gon-na stand be-hind you,

Gon-na, gon-na lead you, soft-ly at the start, gent-ly by the heart, sweet

love! Slip-ping soft-ly to the sea you and me

both mine, won-drous as a green grow-ing for-est vine.

Ba-by, when I find you, Nev-er gon-na stand be-hind you.

Gon-na, gon-na lead you. Soft-ly at the start, gent-ly by the heart, sweet

love! Ba-by, when I find you....